BURNING TOWN

BY
M.C. CARLSON

Dedicated to my wife, Lisa, for challenging me to write a book and for sending me out of the country to get it done.

And, to all the bullies out there for providing the fuel needed for writing- Back at you.

Chapter I-

She didn't say anything. He didn't either. Clay Morris sat across from them at the large cafeteria table. Like a skeptic, he looked at the pair of young teens who had just watched him finish his glass of orange juice without saying a word. *Those two outcasts wouldn't say anything*, he thought. Instead, it was the cackle of the boys standing restlessly behind him that did the telling. He understood immediately what their laughter meant and his scowling brow gave away his feeling of anxiety. Jason and William were nearly hysterical with laughter, and the reason for their boisterousness was whatever had given Clay's drink its strange taste. He had finished the glass and unknowingly must have swallowed something terrible, for it was the act of finishing that last gulp of his drink that had set the two off.

"He did it!" Jason hooted.

"I know. I can't believe he actually did it. This is gonna be awesome," William echoed.

Again, Clay looked to the faces of the kids sitting across from him for insight into what had happened. Whatever had occurred, it had only taken a matter of a few seconds when Clay had left his lunch unguarded while he had gotten up to toss some junk in the trashcan. He stared at them across the expanse of the table. The acne-faced boy looked away, refusing to get involved. The heavyset girl, with a rat's nest of hair that made her look as though she had just climbed out of bed, lowered her eyes.

"I'm sorry," she said sheepishly. She began to gently shake her head from side to side indicating her disapproval. She shook it again disappointed for not being able to speak up. Clay hadn't really expected them to say anything- why would they? They had all been victimized by this same group of boys themselves at least once before and nobody had been there to help them either. They, and anyone else including Clay sitting at the outcast table, were the victims of bullying and they had been conditioned to uphold their vows of silence.

Clay stood up from the table, mustering up all the inner strength he had, and took his cafeteria tray to the garbage can. Jason and William scurried away attempting not to bust at the seams with laughter. As he scraped the rest of his plate of cold French fries into the trash and placed his tray on the large metal rack of dirty dishes, he noticed a few remnants of some white grainy substance at the bottom of his glass that once spilled over with orange juice. Snickers and giggles from other students in the room quietly beckoned a reaction, but they would not be rewarded.

The young man turned, held his head high and let his gaze wander with his thoughts to a place where they could not touch him. He began to walk past Jason and William on his way out of the cafeteria- they had strategically positioned themselves in front of the room's only exit back into the heart of the school. William poked out his foot just as Clay walked by. It was just enough to catch his toe so that he staggered and had to put his hand on the floor to prevent him from completely falling on his face as they had wished he would. The crowd giggled again and Jason bellowed with laughter. Recovering from the trip, Clay escaped the room.

That was enough for today. It was only lunch hour, but Clay Morris had nothing left. The energy consumed while trying to keep his composure in the face of his enemies with the school watching was too much to bear and he decided to forego visiting his locker and signing out at the front office as he left the building. His absence wouldn't be noticed anyway and he was certain he would not be missed.

It's a good thing that he left when he did too because it was only minutes after he arrived home that it happened. The substance that he had consumed in his drink was obviously a laxative; an over-the-counter drugstore purchase from his tormentors. His stomach walls churned the fluids within the way an unexpected tsunami would destroy an otherwise calm bay. Clay didn't even bother to kick off his shoes when he attempted to quietly enter his house. With his dad at work and his mom locked away in her room, he went unnoticed bolting up the stairs to the washroom; clenching the entire way. He tried to silence the door to the bathroom as he closed it, but in his haste, it shut, slamming noisier than he had planned.

He hoped his mother wouldn't hear it and come to check on him. He was not supposed to be home from school and he absolutely did not want her to send him back. Clay paused and held his breath for a moment listening for her footsteps in the house.

Either Mrs. Morris didn't hear the door, or she chose to ignore it; both situations were equally likely.

The cramping in his bowels made him refocus. He dropped his pants and seated himself on the toilet, pain from the swelling and bloating seemed to twist a knife in his insides. It was as though demons had been conjured from the underworld and Clay's belly was doing its best to expel them. He doubled over in pain, resting his head on his knobby bare knees. *What if my life doesn't get any better than this?* he wondered. Clay cried as he rode out the violent storm within his stomach. An agonizing couple of hours rounded out an average day for Clay and he eventually retreated, lost for energy, to his bedroom for the night.

Chapter II-

The fires grew closer last night; closer than they had been in days past. And there was nothing anyone could do about it. Clay dreamt of the fires often, but last night they consumed his thoughts and he woke in a sweat. His short, chestnut colored hair was rarely brushed and the prominent freckles on his soft pale cheeks made him appear a lot younger than sixteen. He was lean and taller than most kids his age and the fact that the thickest parts of his appendages were his knee and elbow joints, made him look a bit like a walking stick bug when he climbed out of bed and clumsily made his way over to his dresser to find some clothes for school.

The sun made the mistake of rising early, Clay thought. It seemed to climb into the sky sooner than normal and with the eagerness and hue that suggested it should be the beginning of a bright new day. It had made a mistake though. This was not the start of a day anyone would want to remember; anyone except for Clay. He had waited a long time for this day. Today was the day when he would start his journey toward getting out of this hellhole town.

The smell of burning was a common one for Clay in the late summer and early autumn. Pine Creek was surrounded by forests and often the sky at this time of year would be filled with ashes from forest fires flaring up off in the distance. The sinister, smoky aroma of the burning of nearby trees caused his eyes to water.

For the past couple of years, Clay Morris had been attending Pine Creek Community High School where he was routinely issued dismal report cards showing cumulative averages in all of his courses in the upper forties and lower fifties, with the exception of his biology mark which sat at approximately sixty-one percent. The only number higher than his grade in science was his total number of unexcused absences from classes, which sat boldly at a combined 62 with two months left in the school year. Not once had Clay's parents ever received a call home about his progress or the lack thereof. This was Pine Creek School and mediocrity was acceptable. In fact, walking the fine line between passing and being kicked out of school meant that you were an average kid. Clay was not average though, nor would it seem that way to anyone willing to take the time to get to know him. The trouble was nobody ever did. As it was on any typical day, he went about his business in obscurity, keeping a low profile, never alluding to the fact that he had so much more to offer. He kept quiet about the fact that school work, as it was presented in class, was so ridiculously easy that it bored him and thus, he just didn't bother to do most of his assignments. So it was quite strange that this morning, as close as he was to failing out of school, one of his science teachers, Mr. Kent, had requested that he be tested for giftedness.

The way it all came about was a bit by chance. With Clay's marks in school as bleak as they were, there was no way it would strike anyone that he was gifted. However, Mr. Kent caught Clay on film one day, and the story he saw unravel on the video footage had a very different plot.

For the past year or so, Mr. Kent had been the victim of thefts from his office in the hallway on the top floor of the high school. It started with his name plate being pried from the door and then, a few days later, the doorknob itself was stolen. Eventually the thieves, whoever they were, grew tired of stealing Mr. Kent's name plate and they started breaking into his office by removing the screws holding the doorknob in place. After gaining access to his small private quarters, they would steal either his electric pencil sharpener or stapler. Often the stolen merchandise would show up days later in another section of the school in a toilet or fountain. Once, the brazen pilferers had gone so far as to run his hole punch up the school's flag pole for all to admire.

He had complained about the thievery to the school administration several times to no avail; this result was fairly typical when anyone, including students or parents, would approach the school's senior administration with concerns.

Mr. Kent was a tall and slender gentleman with a head full of bristly white hair that often had a mind of its own and stood out on one side of his head as if he had been walking in a strong wind. He never raised his voice; however, when he spoke, his deep tone and British accent demanded everyone within ear shot listen with undivided attention. Being an older, weathered man with little patience, he had had enough of the shenanigans and eventually took the matter of defending his office into his own hands.

7

Mr. Kent had placed a motion sensing video camera outside his office. The state-of-the-art device looked nothing of the sort. It was clunky and black and looked like an old smoke alarm or bell system on the ceiling tiles in the hallway. Its ordinary look was the reason he bought the model he did; he was hoping it would remain unnoticed.

Cameras like this one reacted when they detected motion in their fields of view. It would begin to record as soon as it sensed movement and after the motion had ceased for a minute or two, it would shut itself off. This particular model had a built-in timer so that it would rewind and reset whenever it got to the end of the reel of tape, which took a day's worth of film if left to continuously record. Mr. Kent never let it get to the end of a roll of tape though, as he set it up so that it would only activate at the end of each day when most students would be out of the building and there was never enough motion in the hallway throughout the night to keep it recording long enough to reset itself.

Routinely, he would only capture the janitors working or a few kids who showed up to get something out of their lockers at the last minute like a forgotten football or cell phone. There was so little action in the upper hallway of the Annex that it took five or six days to fill the reel of tape before it would reset. Usually, Mr. Kent would have screened the footage before then. The camera's lens had a view of the entire length of the hallway, which included a row of faculty offices alternating with a selection of classrooms.

Few kids ventured up to this part of the building unless their lockers were located in that hallway or they had a class held in one of the rooms. In any case, this was not where the cool kids hung out. Even Jason, the self-proclaimed coolest kid in the world, didn't spend much time in this hallway; he would pretty much just get his stuff out of his locker and head back down to the cafeteria where he hung out with the rest of his jackass buddies.

The camera would catch any movement day or night and Mr. Kent intended to get the thieves on film. He would sit in his office sipping a coffee and review the tape about once a week by fast forwarding through the footage. Nothing of interest to Mr. Kent had been found during the film screenings; that is until recently, when he caught Clay Morris on tape.

Clay rarely went into the upstairs hallway himself. But every once in a while, if he was having a particularly bad day, he would hideout at the end of the hallway and read, knowing it was unlikely anyone would be there to bother him. There was some solace in this. Clay would grab a couple of twelfth grade textbooks that had been left behind in the school library by some of his careless peers and work through them. Sometimes, he would read through classic novels or books on the history of modern warfare, while other days, he would get lucky and find physics or mathematics books. When this happened, he'd sit there in the hallway doing all of the problems by hand on scrap sheets of paper.

It was fun for him and the personal challenge of figuring out the material without any instruction was rewarding. After finishing a substantial section of one of these texts, he'd toss the working papers in the nearby trashcan and head back down to his next period course. It was his way of recharging, of calming down, or of getting psyched up for his next class; especially if it was going to be one with Jason in it. It was this activity that had been caught on Mr. Kent's video recorder.

Mr. Kent had arrived at school one Monday morning eager to check through the past week's film with hopes of catching the thieves at work. After screening through hours of footage, he eventually came across a section of tape showing Clay at a distance, marking up some textbooks with a pen before tossing them in a rusted-out locker with its door barely attached to the hinges. To Kent, as he watched it unfold on the flickering computer screen in his office, it appeared as a fairly standard act of vandalism by one of the brats at Pine Creek School and he assumed Clay had just filled the books with dirty drawings or profanity.

When he eventually went into the hallway and dug through the locker to retrieve the damaged texts, he learned otherwise. Clay had actually been correcting some other kid's homework in an advanced chemistry workbook. The teen captured on film had stolen the book from a lab bench when it was left in a classroom and he was in the process of balancing some of the Redox reactions in it, fixing the other student's errors. He had worked through each question, meticulously recording his steps in the margins of each page. He had eventually tossed the lab book and the accompanying textbook into the empty locker. Mr. Kent had found the workbook and quickly realized that Clay was not the dummy he was perceived to be.

After doing some further inquiring with Clay's teachers, Kent found that Clay was the sort of pupil who removed himself from all involvement with other students. He sat at the back of the class, never took notes or became actively engaged in lessons, and only spoke when spoken to by his professors. Mr. Kent, wanting to see how intelligent Clay actually was, eventually requested that Miss Thompson, the school's guidance counselor, run him through a series of tests to assess whether or not he was, in fact, as gifted as the video footage and subsequent investigation would suggest. Ms Thompson was reluctant at first, but Mr. Kent persisted and Clay's parents had been notified about his upcoming assessment.

His parents had little to say about the situation but told him he had to do the test whether he was interested or not. In fact, his father's exact comment, while signing away permission for him to attend the testing appointment, was something along the lines of: "You need to write some smart kid test. Not so sure they got the right kid. Maybe everyone has to do it. Either way, you'd better show up." Clay's father had never really been supportive about anything; especially school. Perhaps this was why Clay rarely put much effort into his studies. In fairness, his father really did respect those with an education and often made sly remarks to Clay like "Doing well enough in school to earn a scholarship will be the only way you're ever gonna go to college- 'cause I sure as hell ain't paying for it."

On the other hand, his dad's own mother, Clay's grandmother, had always said, "Knowledge gained from a good education is one of the most important things in life." This wasn't something Clay was totally sold on, but he did like being able to argue with people when he knew he had the knowledge to back it up. For the past few years of Clay's teenage life, most arguments tended to be with his father. So, when Mr. Morris had made the comment about them not getting "the right kid," Clay took the remark as a personal challenge.

Clay had a shower and got dressed in some blue jeans that would have been cool had the fit from ten years ago come back in style- but, they had not come back in style. Nor had his favorite T-shirt which he threw on for the third straight day. A faded tone of washed grey, the shirt had a screened image of Sam Cooke at the Harlem Club in 1963 and the name of one of his biggest hits, "*A Change is Gonna Come*," written across the back shoulder line in white stylized font. With the narrowness of his shoulders, the slogan on the shirt seemed to have the first and last letters fold in on themselves making the phrase illegible. It had been handed down to him from one of his uncles who owned a struggling music shop in the city. At the time, Clay didn't know anything about Sam Cooke, so he had gone to the local library and listened to a few of his albums on an old record player. He had been hooked ever since.

Clay strayed downstairs into the kitchen. The room was quiet as usual. His father was already at work and his mother was back in her room where she would spend most of the morning. He didn't really feel like eating breakfast, but figured he might need some brain food for the test. So, he sat down and quickly choked down the blandness of what seemed to be processed cardboard flakes.

He put his dishes in the sink, grabbed his music player and earphones and headed out the door to catch the bus which had been patiently waiting at the end of the street. Clay staggered down his front steps, across the lawn and out toward the sidewalk. He didn't usually take the bus, as the school really wasn't that far from home if he took the shortcut through the woods, but today he was running a bit late and did not really feel like walking. As he stepped on board, Ms Williams, the tired and unfriendly driver, nodded and waited for him to take his seat in the front row. No other kids ever sat in the front row. The closest kids were at least four or five rows behind and the progression of perceived coolness increased with each row moving back. As the bus began to lurch forward, a crumpled ball of paper bounced off the back of Clay's head.

Why me? he thought as he slid further down in his seat, put his earphones on and pushed PLAY. *A Change is Gonna Come* drowned out the noise of the bus.

When the bus arrived at school, Clay was the first off. It wasn't as though he was overly excited to start this school day in late September of his junior year- after all, the way it started seemed pretty typical for him; however, today he had a feeling in the pit of his stomach that something was different.

Clay hurried across the lawn riddled with pine cones and into the Annex building to his locker. Though the Annex was far removed from the main school building, he felt safer there. To get to the Annex one would have to leave the main building from the end nearest the gymnasium and walk under a paved covered walkway several hundred feet long. The covered walkway was supposed to give kids shelter during the winter but the blowing snow often ended up concealing it with snowdrifts and nobody ever shoveled it. Now this isolated part of the school housed the health class, some science labs and a couple vocational workshops.

Classes in this wing were labeled with a number followed by the letter A, for Annex. The kids housed here were their own breed and most had some kind of label also. Stereo-types were well supported as the metal and woodworking kids followed in their fathers' footsteps and the few science-minded kids at Pine Creek usually kept their heads in the books to avoid being abused too badly by the rest of the student body.

Although most kids were able to stay out of trouble, Clay was regularly bullied by Jason Blithe. Any time Jason wasn't picking on Clay, he would watch him the same way a predator watches its prey; looking for the most appropriate time to strike. With all the time Jason had invested in observing Clay, he had begun to notice how truly bright the awkward kid was. As rare as the occurrence had been, Jason had made a mental note each time he had witnessed firsthand how quickly Clay would get his school work done when he actually wanted to. He, on the other hand, came from a long line of uneducated Blithes. He struggled with grasping concepts covered in class and, even though no one else seemed to be aware of Clay's abilities, deep inside he grew jealous of this scrawny kid who actually had enough intellectual potential to get out of town. It made him even more resentful knowing Clay was wasting his talents.

Jason Blithe and his cronies in grade eleven, most of who fit in fairly well in the workshop setting, ventured to this wing of the school more seldom than one would expect.

At the moment, they were hanging out in the heart of the main building where there was always more going on. Jason's friends were crowded around him as if his self-declared popularity was magnetic. Billy and Mark buzzed about him hanging on his every word. For a junior, Jason was one of those absurdly huge kids that had started shaving by the age of thirteen and he was your typical small town hockey player with dreams of getting out of this town one way or another. At least Clay could appreciate the fact that Jason also wanted out.

Jason sure wasn't going to make it out of Pine Creek because of an academic scholarship. Instead, his hopes were in playing professional hockey one day. He had been scouted by some big American universities and, as long as he just kept playing the way he was playing and stayed injury free, he would be off to somewhere like Boston College or the University of Michigan on a scholarship. His older brother, Chris Blithe, had gone on to play at the Division I school in Michigan and eventually played some semi-pro hockey overseas for a year or two in Belarus before taking a job as a bouncer at a night club.

Even though he was physically imposing, Jason Blithe wasn't much to look at and he had a hard time getting girls. He was huge; broad shouldered, a thick back and virtually no neck. His wrists were thick as tree trunks and his hands like cinder blocks. This, Clay knew from experience. Jason had definitely honed his hockey fighting skills through years of throwing punches toward Clay and other helpless victims in the school hallways. Jason's face had been scarred from several years' worth of hockey fights; one large crease stretched from his right ear to the side of his mouth. His left ear had been permanently damaged during a fight with his older brother, Chris, resulting in a hematoma, which separated the cartilage from the tissue supplying blood to that part of the ear. The lasting effect for him was a swollen, hardened, deformed tissue the doctors called 'cauliflower ear'. Anyway, the girls in school had taken notice and seemed not to be interested.

Clay, arriving at his locker upstairs in the Annex, spun open his lock, then opened his dented locker door.

Thump. Thump. Thump.

Three tattered textbooks and a bunch of wadded papers spilled out onto the floor. The noise caught the attention of the boy standing two lockers down.

"One of those days?" he said, looking over at Clay.

"It's always one of those days," Clay responded. As he bent down to pick up his stuff, he saw a note that must have also fallen out with the books.

Hey loser   we r watchin u

The other boy could see Clay picking up the note. "Jason?" he asked rhetorically.

"Yeah," Clay said. "I freakin' hate that guy."

"I wouldn't say that too loud. You never know when he's around. Or, the rest of those guys," said the boy as he swung his locker closed and walked away.

"Wherever he is, they better have tutors there," Clay said, crumpling the ball of paper in his fist and cramming the last few things back into his locker. *He's likely downstairs in the main building. I'll have to steer clear of that area*, he thought.

Homeroom and then the test, Clay processed the thought while gathering a few supplies from his locker. *Then, I can skip the afternoon.* He slammed the bright orange, metal door closed, reattached his lock, checked to see that it was secured and entered a classroom close by.

Homeroom was always a challenge. It was only five minutes, but the class rosters were organized alphabetically by last name. Clay's last name was Morris. Jason's was Blithe so he was in a different room and so were a couple of Jason's closest friends, William and Billy. But Jason's other jerk buddies, Nathan McIntire,

17

Mark Mathies, and Leon Nel would all be there in Clay's homeroom ready and willing to wreak havoc. None of them were as bad as Jason, but they were still people Clay wanted to be cautious around. Whether or not Clay would end up in the middle of something with these guys in homeroom was always a crap shoot.

It was a lucky day, no horrific encounters with the other boys had taken place and the 9:00am bell signaling the end of homeroom period and the start of period one rang loudly in the Annex hallway.

Clay headed out of the Annex, scurrying back and forth between students under the covered walkway like a fish swimming upstream, and into the doors of the main building. He was wise enough to take the first set of stairs by the gym up to the second floor; as using the stairs further down the first floor hallway would have increased his chances of running into Jason. Clay entered the staircase and, as he reached the landing at the top, he passed by a group of girls who were hanging out. It was this moment when she caught his eye for the first time.

"Hey," he said in a barely audible voice as he passed by the group, in part hoping they would recognize his approach and might move out of the way as he went by.

"Hey," she replied back with a slight, quick head gesture upwards acknowledging he was there.

That was a big moment for Clay. Girls rarely spoke to him; usually it was only to ask to borrow paper or a pencil or to tell him to get away from them.

Under the excess of makeup, and the long brown hair that swept across to shade her face, this girl was stunning. She had sculpted eyebrows that met at the top of a thin nose that turned up ever so slightly at the bottom. Her lips were full and red. She had darkened the lower half of her eyelids painting the top with a silvery sheen that gave them an ominous sparkle. And they were looking at him.

He smiled to himself as he bounded up the stairs with a spring that was unfamiliar to him. Optimistic about the recognition from the girl in the staircase, the test and the future it might set him up for, he felt excited. This level of energy was atypical for him and he knew it, but he was mixed up with emotions of excitement and happiness that the morning had gone so well thus far. Aside from the ball of paper hitting him while on the bus and the note in his locker, it had been uneventful in terms of any bullying issues.

For most kids, nothing out of the ordinary happening would mean there was no reason to get excited, but for Clay, it meant he hadn't had his ass kicked by some puck-head hockey player. This didn't happen every single day, but often enough that it was reason to be constantly on edge. The physicality of being punched or choked had lost its bite long ago, but each time it happened, the social and emotional impact of being humiliated in front of others would linger for days.

As he approached the Student Services Centre, he saw Mr. Kent and Ms Thompson approaching down the hallway. He let himself into the room just as the two teachers caught up.

"You ready? Mr. Kent questioned in his baritone voice.

"Yeah, I think so," said Clay.

"Well, I'll get you all set up and you can take a seat in the third study carol. OK, Clay?

"Alright," he said, still trying to recall the image of the girl in the staircase as he headed to the secluded carol in the corner of the room. Clay took a seat and got out his pencils and calculator as Ms Thompson placed a copy of the test on his desk. Mr. Kent popped his head into the carol and wished him luck before moving into the adjacent office belonging to Ms Thompson.

Mr. Kent was a pretty good guy. Though Clay's mark in biology class was his best mark, it was still not up to Mr. Kent's standards. Clay wasn't sure if Mr. Kent didn't like having failing kids in his class because he actually cared about them, or if it was because his personal pride from having his entire class pass each term would be jeopardized. He hoped it was the former. Either way, Mr. Kent was the one and only teacher who had ever called home about his performance at school.

Truth be known, it was Mr. Kent's last year of teaching before retiring and, as with many soon to be retirees, he had done some soul searching. He had been feeling guilty that he had been in a professional rut for the last twenty years of teaching; just going through the motions each day. There hadn't been much of a push from school administration to improve his practice or to professionally develop and he hadn't put any time into it as a result. It seemed as the town had floundered during the last decade, so had the public high school and every teacher and student in it, including Mr. Kent. Knowing there weren't going to be many other opportunities, he thought that, perhaps, saving one more kid could be his way of finishing off his career on a positive note. Thus, this test.

Clay took a moment to read the profanity that had been carved into the study carol by previous owners. Nothing out of the ordinary. Just the standard, "screw this school" type stuff. He traced the letters of the slander scratched into the finish of the desk. *Yeah... Screw this school*, he thought. Clay took a moment to survey the rest of the room around him noting a couple of anti-smoking and Kids Help Phone posters then began writing the test spread out in front of him.

It was known as the Wechsler Intelligence Scale for Children, or the WISC-IV, and it was supposed to be scheduled as a series of subtests, with some parts taking place on different days, but Ms Thompson, being skeptical of the whole ordeal, just wanted Clay to get it over with so she booked him in to do it all in one sitting. She seemed particularly uninterested during the sections she had to administer.

It was relatively easy for Clay; mainly a comprehensive list of questions involving logic, reasoning and understanding. Though there were elements of the test that involved defining terms or describing similarities between pairs of words, it was mainly designed to test a student's potential ability rather than what they already knew. The final section of the test was a supplemental portion specifically requested by Mr. Kent. It was a timed mathematics portion that Clay breezed through with little difficulty.

Upon completing the test, Clay quietly thanked Ms Thompson and Mr. Kent who had been in and out of the room all morning. Then he collected his belongings and left the Student Services Centre slipping down the same staircase he had used earlier in the day, in part hoping she would be there again. She was not.

He pushed the door open and started down a pathway that led to the back of the school where he could cut through the forest on his long walk home. Within a couple of short steps he noticed Jason standing near the path a little ways up ahead.

Oh great. Here we go again, he thought, seeing Jason standing there with Leon and Billy, two of his jackass pals.

Jason saw Clay coming across the path and threw a shoulder into him as he walked by. *That was it?* Clay wondered. He got away easy today.

Chapter III-

Clay Morris grew up in Pine Creek, a modest town of about 40,000 people flanking the north and east side of a large blue-green mountain lake. Pine Lake, as it was called, sat nestled into a valley with substantial rocky mountain peaks on all sides. The town was originally built around ranching and when the railroad came through a hundred years ago it became a real hub for farmers, ranchers, and trappers alike. As years went on, the logging, paper and copper mining industries grew and the town became a city.

The city was barely breathing through the stench of pulp mills that strangled the airways of everyone living in Pine Creek without them even being aware of the slow and steady chokehold they were in. Recent years had passed like a math test: slow and painful.

Times had been rough for Pine Creek and, as it had been in the past, once again many families now found it necessary to hunt for deer and moose or to fish in order to keep food on their tables. Recently, most of the locals struggled to get by, as the softwood lumber disputes with countries logging companies used to export to and the increasing automation of the mine and mills left fewer jobs to go around.

The working-aged people in Pine Creek were all gritty as sandpaper. Their children were a mixed bag. Many of them were even rougher than their parents; making a name for themselves as people you didn't want to say the wrong things to or get caught looking at the wrong way. This wasn't much of a problem for Clay as he detested the guys in town, and the girls often seemed even rougher around the edges than their counterparts, so he avoided them as well. For the most part, he tried to keep his head down and his mouth shut. It was simply a lot safer that way.

The last few years had brought with them a new breed of "homesteaders." As the wilderness had become a place far removed from the major cities in the south, hoards of ecotourists now flooded Pine Creek looking to fill some kind of void they had made in their souls through years of working in concrete jungles. They all thought they could get back to nature in a couple of weekend days by rafting the white water rivers, canoeing the calm lakes, climbing the nearby cliffs, and mountain biking and hiking in wilds that residents of Pine Creek had called their back yards for generations.

When the Olympics were hosted a couple of years ago, by Vancouver, a city about a three hour's drive from Pine Creek, it brought a new level of attention to the area. It was great while it lasted, as it brought a lot of life into the local stores and restaurants for a couple of months. But, nobody expected the intensity of development that was lagging slightly behind.

People around the world had discovered the secret natural beauty of the hidden gem of a town. Foreign investors were smart by capitalizing on the demand. Tour operators and hotel chains quickly sprung up everywhere along the west side of the lake. The beauty of the town was only skin deep though. The success of their ventures had not been shared with the locals and there was a steady stream of bitterness between the jagged miners and loggers and the tour companies.

A jealous tension was building steadily in the town. The rough locals were always under the impression that all of their proposed plans for exploration of new areas to log and mine were being shot down at city council meetings by the lining of aldermen and council member's pockets by the rich CEO's of the ecotourism companies. Alternatively, the CEO's felt that the pristine look of the new territories they had planned for tourism expansion would be negatively impacted by any additional industrial developments.

The granola types really didn't want to see logging next to their campsites. But, they had no problem burning down half the forest in their campfires each night. Where did they think that wood came from that they bought at the local gas stations? Either way, it was perceived that no adventure company would let their progress and cash flow be hindered by more traditional industries.

This aggressive nature spilled into the schools as well. The old, run-down school on the north part of the city housed most of the riff raff. Pine Creek Community High School, as it was so creatively named, was built like a factory of the Industrial Revolution, designed to treat students like material goods in an assembly line getting passed down a conveyer belt hallway from room to room. Each stop along the way was where a new piece of information was added to the creation before being pushed along to the next classroom. Bells ringing hourly signaled the next shipment of students had arrived ready to replace the soon-to-be-forgotten, shabbily assembled products.

No legitimate relationships ever developed between student and teacher. Teachers were just the conveyers of information and students were vessels to be filled. Apparently, there was no money in any provincial or civic budget to renovate or upgrade the crumbling building. The disaster of an educational institution sat tucked back into the forest at the end of a road that nobody in their right mind would ever want to drive down. Yet, a couple of beaten up school buses and hundreds of teenaged, zombie-like walkers made the trip to Pine Creek Community High School each day.

Alternatively, as the wealthy population grew, the need for a new school was evident and the decision to put it where the new homes were being built around the south end of the lake was made in haste. Because this independent school, called Stonebridge Academy, was mainly privately funded by the new eco-industries, it was outrageous; situated right on the shores of Pine Lake with more glass than the scenery could make use of.

There were laboratories and gymnasia that would rival any Ivy League University's, alcoves in the hallways with leather seats and mounted high definition television screens showing images of performances that had recently taken place in the school's large theatre. Band and art rooms were filled with new instruments and easels and students' work was proudly displayed in ornate highlighted cabinetry along the broad corridors. Stonebridge

Academy threw out more resources on a daily basis than Pine Creek Community School was allotted each year.

Alternatively, Clay's school across the city was lucky if it could keep incandescent bulbs in the fixtures or paint from peeling off the walls. There was no artwork at Pine Creek School displayed in the hallways. In fact, there were few things to celebrate in the school's long history. A single athletics trophy case sat near the front entrance. Short on earned supplies to stock it, the case was filled in part with the year-end academic awards and a framed Belarusian ice hockey jersey from a team named Karamin Minsk. The plaque at the bottom of the frame prominently read:

Pine Creek Community School's Own Champion: Chris Blithe

The only other decorations, aside from some poorly displayed student work that was often half torn down or graffitied on, were a plaque that commemorated the opening of the school in 1957 and a picture of the school building itself.

Chapter IV-

The results of the WISC-IV came in a brown envelope sent directly to Clay's house. Mr. Morris had found the letter addressed to him on the bureau in the dining room after coming home late from work one evening. It was standard practice for the school guidance department to share the results of tests like these with parents at a meeting with everyone present. But, Ms Thompson figured that given the lack of interest from Clay's parents, a letter home would suffice.

At the time, Clay was sitting at the dinner table eating a microwaved meal left out for him by his mother. She had left out two plates on the counter and had since returned to her bedroom. In her state of depression, this was all Clay had come to expect.

Come on, come on, come on, Clay pleaded silently, attempting to will his father out of the room so he could read the document for himself. Anxiously tapping his foot against the chair leg, he watched as his dad tore the edge off of the envelope and pulled out the single folded sheet of paper. Clay could see the school's logo embossed at the top of the page as the ceiling light shone through from behind his father. He realized that it was a letter regarding the test, but for fear of drawing more of his dad's attention to what might end up being poor results, he chose not to say anything and just bit his lip as he watched Mr. Morris take a moment to skim through the letter.

"Huh," Mr. Morris said, seemingly confused by the note. He casually tossed the letter on the bureau, then walked back into the kitchen and heated up the second plate of dinner.

Just hurry up and leave already. Clay was growing ever more nervous.

Mr. Morris took the semi-warm dish from the microwave and proceeded to sit in the heavily worn armchair in the neighbouring TV room where he would eat each night while watching the local news.

From where he sat eating, Clay could see his father. Though he desperately wanted to read the letter on the bureau, he would not get up until Mr. Morris was gone. His mind alternated briskly back and forth between focusing on the paper he desperately wanted to read and on choking down the tan-colored gruel scattered across his own plate.

Within ten minutes or so, the news broadcast ended.

"Arrrrumph." Mr. Morris groaned loudly as he stood up from his chair. He placed the empty dinner plate on a nearby coffee table and trudged upstairs.

"Finally!" Clay sprang from the table and grabbed the sheet of paper. Then, he slipped upstairs into his own bedroom where he could read it in private.

Clay read the letter, which went into some background about the test and the administration procedures and then carried on to cite some historical nonsense about how it could be used to show discrepancies between a child's intelligence and his or her performance at school. His eyes skimmed down the page. The test results followed.

They were tabulated by subsection and he could tell by some of the highlighted values that the results were not as he had expected. Clay skipped to the end of the letter where the trends were summarized. The feedback was positive and the results conclusively showed the young man was gifted in multiple cognitive areas. There was a statement made about the Comprehension section, which involved responding to various social situations. It declared this was a bit of a weak point for him, but in each of the remaining sections, he was off the charts.

Added on a yellow sticky note pasted near the bottom of the form, there was also a handwritten personal message from Mr. Kent:

Congratulations Clay. Please take some time in the near future to come and see me to discuss these results. I encourage you to bring along your parents, as they should be part of the discussion.

Mr. Kent.

"There's no way I'm bringing my parents in to the school. Dad didn't seem too interested when he read this anyway," Clay muttered to himself.

It's not really customary to congratulate someone for the results of this sort of test, but Clay would take it anyway. He felt a lump in his throat and fought the urge to let his eyes tear up. Clay hadn't had any positive comments made about him since his brother had passed.

Chapter V-

They were both eleven when Neil was killed. He was hit by a truck while riding his bicycle to a friend's house. Dead on impact. No chance for revival or for his parents to say good bye. His parents loved both of their twin sons but teachers at school were always, 'Neil Morris this' and 'Neil Morris that.'

Neil and Clay were fraternal twins, sharing a birthday and a family name, but aside from that, not a lot else. Neil was athletic and outgoing. He was funny and artistic. Clay was more of an introvert and as a result, he never received the level of attention that his brother did; it was OK though because even Clay looked up to Neil. They were best friends. Neil would always be the one to speak up for Clay and to back him in any dispute with neighborhood kids.

When Neil passed Mrs. Morris took to her bedroom where she too would read to keep her mind off the loss of her son. Reading was her way of forgetting. Except, she read the same few books over and over. She found that by re-reading books, she had some level of control in her life; nothing would ever change and she knew what to expect.

She continued to look after what she thought of as her daily housewife duties the same way she had beforehand; the cooking and cleaning, but the mother in her was long gone; the drugs had taken care of that. Her doctor had prescribed a barrage of anti-depressants which she took sporadically. She didn't have any real intentions of neglecting Clay and she had consciously made a plan to try and wean herself off of the meds, but she failed to realize that years were casually slipping by in the meantime.

Clay had lost hope in his mother. She seldom spoke to him and it had been at least four years since she had hugged him or kissed his cheek. Mr. Morris never was much more than a provider, but he too became a little more reclusive after it happened and Clay got the impression that his father had resented the fact that it was Neil who had been killed by the driver of the truck and not Clay. The whole situation made things very lonely for Clay.

Chapter VI-

The following morning, Clay could smell the scent of burning lingering in the air again as he left his house. He chose to ride the bus to school and once again he sat alone near the front. This time, three crumpled balls of paper were thrown at him; the first glancing off of his shoulder, the second narrowly missed his head and hit the front windshield of the bus. The driver scolded the kids in the back and told them to stop horsing around or she would pull over. The students knew it was a hollow threat. The third hit him in the back of the neck and fell onto the seat behind him. He did not turn around. They were out of paper to throw.

Clay stepped off the bus and scanned the schoolyard for Jason and his gang. They were not there. He took a deep breath and proceeded into the school where, sure enough, they were present, eagerly awaiting to greet him just inside the doors.

"Hey loser," Billy said.

Jason chimed in with "Fucking Tree Hugger." The designation of Tree Hugger was regularly used derogatively at Pine Creek School, most often in reference to the rich kids from Stonebridge Academy because their family finances were based on ecotourism. Leon, Jason's friend, yelled something else out as Clay walked by, but, by then, Clay had already tuned them out.

Clay skipped his locker and went straight to homeroom. He sat down at one of the tables awaiting roll call. Nathan and Leon tossed a note on Clay's desk as they scrambled in. Clay looked over at the teacher getting up from behind her chair at the front counter to see if she noticed. She did. She always did. And she knew something was up between him and the other boys. But of course, she wouldn't do anything about it. No one could really blame her. After all, they never really did anything too bad in class.

This is the problem with bullying in schools. Most of what happens to the victim happens outside of the class environment. Sure, a bully often makes initial contact with his victim in class because this is where kids spend a large amount of their time. Just the sheer fact that the victim has to spend substantial chunks of time in the close quarters of these classrooms with their tormenters is bad enough, but the parents and educators expect them to learn something while they're there. The precarious situation of constantly living in fear is not really conducive to learning. There are often verbal or written threats made in classrooms or on buses, but typically, most of the more aggressive acts of violence between a bully and his victim happen outside of these so-called "safety zones." Even if his teacher did say something to Nathan and Leon for passing a derogatory note, she would likely be accused by their parents of being too hard on the boys and for not having any concrete evidence that something bad had been happening.

Because of the lack of support, being picked on was something Clay had gotten used to over time. He had ratted some of the instigators out once in middle school. In the end, the school counselor at the time wanted Clay to sit down with his bullies and work on building better relationships. Clay wasn't able to turn the other cheek as the counsellor had hoped- both of his cheeks had been pummelled already anyway.

This is what educators called "restorative treatment." As if a positive relationship between a victim and his bully ever existed to be restored. This double-edged, damned if you do tell someone, damned if you don't, sword was troublesome for Clay. He didn't really want to become friends with the person who had just kicked his ass. He always hoped his homeroom teacher would stand up for him and do something to remove him from the trouble he was in. Unfortunately, it was not to be and as a result, Clay knew to simply keep his mouth shut and hope for the best.

Clay looked down at the note from Nathan and Leon. The folded paper was sitting on the table next to his binders and he could make out Nathan's sloppy printing on the loose leaf sheet. Nathan was a straight up moron. He had the dirtiest glasses anyone had ever seen. It was a wonder he could possibly see through the smears on the lenses. Nathan McIntire was tall and lean but muscular and aged beyond his years.

Leon was nothing of the sort. He was athletic too, but a bit smaller. Girls found him nice to look at and he sure had his share, but once they found out what he was really like, any chance of a relationship vanished.

Mark must have been away sick. Clay could read most of the note without having to pick it up.

Why don't you get your whore of a mother to do some laundry so you don't have to wear the same shirt every day?

Clay looked down at his chest. *A Change is Gonna Come*, he thought.

P.S. I did your mom last night, the note concluded.

As the bell signalling the end of homeroom rang, Clay got up and threw the note in the garbage.

He headed up to Mr. Kent's office where he found the old man sitting at his desk. A number of dirty coffee mugs and a pile of unmarked papers were scattered across the surface in front of him.

"Good morning, Clay."

"Good morning," he responded.

"As you know, the results of the WISC test came in and though they were promising, they showed an alarming trend."

At first Clay wasn't sure where he was going with this, but he quickly understood.

"I feel it's best if I'm just frank with you son. Your marks are pretty horrendous at this point. Yet, you are obviously a smart kid. I know you have been doing a lot of independent studying." Mr. Kent went on to explain how he had caught him on film working in the upper floor hallway outside his office with a motion sensor camera.

Clay thought the whole idea of being spied on with a camera a bit creepy, but he let the thought go.

"So, where to from here? What are your plans?"

Clay didn't really know what to say. He knew what he wanted. He wanted nothing more than to get out of Pine Creek School and Pine Creek forever and this is what he told the teacher who sat listening intently as Clay described his situation. Clay didn't expect to be in this condition, explaining his thoughts and feelings to a man who was practically a stranger to him, but the fact that, for some reason, Mr. Kent seemed genuinely interested in his well-being was comforting. His parents didn't seem to care, but here was an adult who did. It felt soothing as he decompressed by pouring his heart out. He told him about how his brother had died and ever since his parents had been ignoring him. He explained how he was regularly teased by kids at school and how he had no real friends. How he tried to stay away from school to avoid being hurt. How when he had to be at school, he would try to keep his head down and that meant not getting involved in his classes or sticking out by doing well academically. He even told Kent about how he would love to have a girlfriend to talk to one day. Mr. Kent sympathised with Clay and felt sorry for not noticing; rather, for not caring up until now.

Mr. Kent could see the turmoil Clay had been living with. *Jesus, this kid has issues,* he thought. *I've got to help him somehow.*

Obviously, he could not suggest that Clay run away from it all. Nor could he see any chance that Clay's family would be moving to another town. At the very least, he could surely devise a way for him to get away from his current situation but it would take some time. Mr. Kent sat leaning to one side in his chair, rocking it slowly back and forth, and thinking of a strategy to best help the sad case that had poured his heart out in his office.

He spoke calmly, "Clay, I will try my best to help."

"Thank you sir," Clay responded.

"Give me some time to sort some things out and come see me in my office again in a few days' time. OK?"

"Yes sir." Even without physical contact, Clay felt warmed and comforted by the interaction. He quietly left the office and made his way to his next class.

Mr. Kent sat rocking in his desk chair. He couldn't stop thinking, *Not a lot of time before I'm finished here for good. I have to make sure this one turns out alright. I've wasted too many good years not doing enough for these kids. Is there even enough time before June?* Mr. Kent stopped the chair from rocking as he repeatedly questioned himself. *I'll never forgive myself if I don't help.*

It wasn't long before Mr. Kent had constructed a way to help and when the student returned for the follow up meeting a few days later, he explained how there may be some potential for Clay to switch schools. The teacher cleverly devised a deal with the young man.

"Clay, you're going to have to push yourself academically all year," he told the teen. "We'll have to get you enrolled in the advanced classes here in order for you to have a shot at any scholarship for next year. Because without one," he continued, "there will be no way for you to switch schools."

Clay knew there was only one other school in town he could be referring to. Attending Stonebridge Academy had never crossed Clay's mind, but he knew anywhere had to be better than Pine Creek Community High School.

Clay began to worry. "There's no way my family can pay the tuition." Clay also knew his parents didn't understand the dire situation he was in either.

"That's why we have to get your marks up," Mr. Kent explained. "They won't even look at an application from you if you don't start to demonstrate what I believe you are capable of. Would your parents be alright with you taking classes somewhere else?"

Clay's eyes wandered to the floor. "My father certainly wouldn't care and my mom wouldn't even notice."

Mr. Kent could sense the urgency in Clay's voice. "Some changes to your schedule would need to happen starting tomorrow. We'll need to get you into some more demanding courses. Are you up for it?"

"Yes sir, but isn't it too late?"

Mr. Kent went on, "The course change deadline has just passed but I can pull a couple strings and, with Ms Thomson's recent assessment, we'll be able to proceed."

Clay was ecstatic with the thought. Kent would ensure that the registrar made the appropriate changes to his courses and promised he would try and watch over the bullying issue, though Clay knew this was not possible. Eventually, if Clay could keep his grades up, he could apply for a scholarship to Stonebridge Academy. Mr. Kent discussed how students from private schools like Stonebridge got noticed and were more likely to be accepted into universities. This was true even if one ignored the argument that their academic standings were usually better than any of the students from Pine Creek Community High School.

There was something to be said about bumping shoulders with the right folks. Most of the families from Stonebridge had serious connections with the universities in the big city and virtually all of them were major financial donors. Because of this, almost any student with letters of recommendation from the faculty at Stonebridge was accepted. Mr. Kent, being a long standing teacher in the area had his own significant connections at Stonebridge.

Clay knew this was a long shot, but he had no other options. It was either he tough it out for one more year at Pine Creek, or he roll over and die. He had heard Kent's proposal and mulled over the options. *I might as well be dead if I plan on staying at Pine Creek School.* He could see there was no way he could spend a lifetime in this town.

"You will have to take higher level science and math courses, drop any chance of having a spare period, and pick up a second language option to make it work," Mr. Kent explained.

"Do you think I can manage?" Clay asked.

"It doesn't matter what I think, Clay. You're the one who's going to have to do the work."

Clay agreed to make the necessary course switches and to try his best to attain an Honors Standing in each of his classes.

Mr. Kent extended his hand towards Clay. The teen, a bit reluctantly at first, grabbed a hold of Mr. Kent's hand and shook firmly. "I'll go clarify this with Ms Thomson and then I'll speak with the registrar. You, head off to class."

Clay left the office. His mind swirled as he tried to keep up with what was happening. He wasn't sure he was up for the challenge, but someone had taken an interest in him and that little bit of support seemed enough to prompt him into agreeing with every suggestion made. He figured, *At least in the advanced classes, there will be no way I'll share a class with Jason or any of his friends. I'll just have to lay low outside of class time.*

Chapter VII-

A short time had passed since Clay's courses had been changed and he was beginning to get into the groove of his studies. Clay walked down the dismal corridor that led to the library; always watching that one of the cronies wasn't going to jump out from behind the recessed areas where the broken water fountains were tucked into the walls.

The library doors were closed when he got there. He took a moment to admire the new graffiti someone had brazenly carved with a pocketknife into the wooden panel of the door. It read: "Die Fuking nerds and kill all teachrs!! We r Coming 4 U!" Clay shook his head. *The idiots can't even spell.*

Maintenance and cleaning staff were rarely available to clean up things like this as their hours had been drastically cut and they were often so backlogged with repairing fountains filled with gum and chewing tobacco, broken light fixtures or heaters. This particular message would likely stay here until the next summer when the overworked and underpaid staff could finally get to it.

Clay hesitated for a moment and then pushed the door open. It was difficult at first as it caught on the hallway floor, but then it swung freely when the base of the door passed into the area that had worn a scrape into the linoleum tiles. The door had misaligned with its hinges as the building had shifted and weathered over the years.

He walked into the library, half of which looked as though it had been converted into storage for the maintenance department. Un-shelved books were stacked messily on top of the bookcases. In each instance, it was because either the shelf had broken or because there simply was no librarian to put them away after use. Her job had been axed last year in an effort to save money to heat the place. Teachers were supposed to help out with shelving but that never seemed to occur and nobody monitored it.

There was an empty table in a corner which he scurried over to. The orange plastic chairs were often covered in gum, but the gum on the chair he had chosen had long dried and lost its stickiness so he sat on it anyway. He placed his stuff on the table and flipped his book open.

A short while later, the boisterousness of Mark and Billy's voices could be heard coming into the library. Mark was a fairly stocky kid with a serious under bite; not something his parents could afford to fix. Billy, smaller, strawberry blond hair and freckled was an excitable kid when he wasn't medicated. The two came tumbling around a corner, knocking each other into shelves for fun. Following closely behind, were Jason and a couple of girls, one of whom was Dallas Hilton, the girl who had smiled at him in the staircase days ago.

"Hey Faggot!" Mark bellowed. The other boys made similar comments.

"No, it's the Tree Hugger." Jason declared. His friends laughed in approval. Clay looked up at the group and then looked down at his book. They tossed their backpacks on the floor and sat at a nearby table. He couldn't muster the courage to get up and leave, but he soon realized he should have. Clay scanned the room for an adult. The librarian, sat out of earshot behind a counter at the far end of the library. The girls sat chatting about a night they had spent at the movie theater and lies they had told their parents to extend their curfews, while Jason, Mark and Billy talked about the girls as if they weren't in the same room. Other students casually flowed in and out of the library unaware of the tension that was heavy in the room.

How the hell am I gonna get out of this one? Clay stayed true to his plan of keeping his head down while waiting for the right moment when the others were too deep in conversation to notice him get up and leave. Just as the boys began laughing hysterically about some rude sexual remark one of them had made, Clay made his decision that it was time he bolt. *Now or never,* he thought. Clay was just starting to pack up his books and papers, when at that very moment he noticed William walking in to join the crew and he decided against leaving. William pulled up a chair from a nearby table making sure to cause a scene by banging it around and knocking into Mark as he did so.

Shoot! Now what am I supposed to do? Clay was stuck. Subtlety, he scanned the library looking for alternate exits, but found none amidst the shelves of books. For a while it seemed that they had forgotten he was in the room. They went on about their sexual exploits. Clay was shocked to hear about what the girls were willing

45

to do at parties and how the boys seemed to abuse the girls' needs for acceptance. Mark blurted about how he had received oral sex from some girl at a party and that he was too drunk to even know who it was. Apparently the girl was too drunk also.

Jason bragged, "You guys shoulda seen this girl I was with yesterday at lunch hour in the forest behind the school." He carried on speaking as if the girl he had been with was a wild animal he had tamed. "She was so freaking hot for me." He used words that demonstrated little respect for women in general.

"Whatever," Mark said, questioning the authenticity of his story.

"Nobody would do you in broad daylight," laughed William as he kicked Jason's shin under the table. Jason threw a pencil back hitting William square in the chest. Billy, who had observed Clay at the nearby table attempting to remain unnoticed, turned toward Clay leaning in to ask, "What about you faggot? You had any pussy lately?"

Jason wanted to get involved and piped up, "That nerd would never get any pussy."

"More than you," Clay lied under his breath.

"I get it any time I want," said Jason.

"Ya, your mom's." Clay surprised himself with the response. His eyes blinked slowly, for a moment wishing he could recall that last statement. But he knew it was too late. By the time he opened them again, Jason had sprung out of his chair and grabbed him by the nose. Jason's thick knuckles wrapped around the cartilage of his nose and yanked his head to the side, jarring his neck. Water began to well up in Clay's eyes. He couldn't stop the tears. He was more worried that the other students who were now watching in the library would tell everyone he was crying than he was about them seeing him getting tugged around by his nose. But he was not crying. The tears were only as a natural reflex to the breaking of the cartilage that formed his once straight nose. Jason pulled up and down with a vice grip honed from years of holding a hockey stick. It was as though Jason was a music conductor waving his fist around in front of himself; Clay still firmly in his grasp.

The ringing in Clay's ears began to get louder.

BRRRIIIINNNNGGGGGG!

At first, he thought it was just from the pain of his broken nose, but then he realized it was a fire alarm going off in the school. Some kid wanting to get out of an afternoon exam figured his best chance was to pull one of the alarms in the hallway. Jason released his grip and the group of them grabbed their bags and started to make for the door.

"Next time watch your mouth, Fuckin' Tree Hugger."

Dallas looked at him as she walked by. Only she didn't smile this time. She just mouthed what looked like the words, "I'm Sorry" as she turned away and followed her friends. Clay stood there for a moment ashamed; his face glowing red with the heat caused by blood welling up in his crooked nose. Then he picked up his things and in an attempt to save face, headed outside to his homeroom's emergency meeting place trying to ignore the pain throbbing in his head.

Clay, humiliated, stood with his head bowed down out in the rain. He slid his way to the back of his homeroom group trying to blend in with the crowd and avoid being noticed by his teacher and peers. He sniffled as a drop of blood, watered down from rain on his face, ran from his nose to his upper lip. Using the back of his hand, he wiped it, not bothering to look at the blood that now covered his knuckles. The blood flowed more freely now and dripped in a steady rhythm onto the ground and his shirt. Clay turned away from the line of students and walked home through the trail system that created a fairly direct route through the forest.

Chapter VIII-

Each day brought new adventures and terrors for Clay. Advanced classes in English literature and physics were found to be quite interesting and he worked hard to stay involved in class discussions. It was easier for him to succeed academically than he had expected it to be; especially in the enriched courses where one wouldn't find the likes of Jason or any of his friends.

Sitting toward the front of each class, he paid close attention to the words of his teachers and did his best to translate them into meaningful notes in his binders. He did still have a couple of courses like health and history where he would occasionally run into the other unwanted crowd. Adding note taking to his in-class activities and studying each night at home, he felt confident in his coursework and regularly earned top marks in his class.

The academic highlights were often overshadowed with interactions between him and Jason or any one of Jason's other friends. Although none of them good, those incidents involving the ringleader were always the worst.

Months passed and Clay stuck to his deal with Mr. Kent who would check in with him at least once a week to see if he was doing alright. Clay always responded that things were, "Fine." Somehow Mr. Kent knew they weren't always okay and he would often pass along a new book for Clay to read for leisure to take his mind off of things. The books were fascinating but they never completely took away the aches of new bruises or the sting of the constant name calling. Often Kent would highlight key passages that were particularly motivating or pose intriguing questions to Clay by writing them in the margins. More than Mr. Kent would ever know, Clay appreciated the communication.

Given that this would be Kent's final year of teaching, there were a lot of issues he just didn't seem to care about or bother with anymore. However, Clay's situation was not something he was going to ignore.

It was the bureaucracy of the school system that really got to him. As the two met one day in the spring, the professor began to talk about his friend, Mr. Cooper, who also worked in the Annex building. He mentioned that Mr. Cooper, one of the school's new chemistry and health teachers, needed to take a day off one Friday to deal with some personal matters.

Apparently, Mr. Cooper was in the midst of a divorce. He explained how there was no way he should be calling in sick for personal matters again as he had been scolded by his administrators for what had occurred the last time.

The substitute teacher he had booked to relieve him during his absence had been horrific, letting the class get wildly out of control, and then, in an attempt to settle the masses, the sub had chosen to project a movie he found on the internet instead of teaching the fairly simple lesson that Mr. Cooper had left for him. The principal, who happened to be walking down the hall, had heard the commotion and decided to pop his head in the room just in time to see half the class asleep with their heads on their desks and the other half sitting in a stupor watching some Hollywood comedy with no educational significance whatsoever. It was just a case of bad timing. And bad subbing.

Good subs were nearly impossible for teachers at Pine Creek School to find. Rarely, did administration ever venture far enough through the halls of the main school to actually make their way to the Annex building to see it for themselves. Though Mr. Cooper needed to be away from class on Friday, he was worried about how things would unfold and he didn't have the emotional willpower to deal with administration about it again. Kent went on to explain, "I believe Mr. Cooper is a great young teacher having a tough time with his family life."

Unfortunately, Clay didn't give a rat's ass about Cooper's family life.

"Besides," Mr. Kent said, "The class couldn't afford to waste another period watching movies with a substitute teacher this close to the end of the year. Mr. Cooper needs to have a good showing with his classes on the summative year-end exams or he'll be let go this summer. He doesn't yet have his permanent teaching certification."

The next request took Clay by surprise. "I really need you to step up and be a leader in this class. You need to support the substitute, whoever it ends up being. The class has to be kept under control. We can't afford to let good teachers go around here."

The young student was taken aback. His ears perked up and he listened as his teacher explained how he knew the class was just working on a small assignment and then listening to presentations that day so it wouldn't involve them doing any real instructional lessons. Clay was up for the challenge but still, he showed reluctance when the agreement was made because he knew there were other individuals in that class who had the potential to derail the whole agenda.

On Friday, Clay showed up in Mr. Cooper's classroom in the Annex building and found a stack of worksheets on the teacher's desk that had been left for the sub, a frazzled looking, waif-like old lady who had just slipped in unnoticed and was currently hanging her purse and jacket on the back of Mr. Cooper's desk chair.

That stack of papers must be the assignment Mr. Kent had referred to, Clay thought to himself as he strode over to his own desk near the back. The substitute was to get the other students through the worksheet and then organize them so that they could each present an oral report on some health issue impacting teenagers. No real teaching was happening, but the substitute teacher had been asked by Mr. Cooper to formatively assess the work of the class.

Clay understood this meant the work wasn't really going to count for much on any report card, but the rest of the kids didn't know that.

The lady tried to calm down the students who were choosing to stand around chatting with their friends instead of taking their seats.

These darn kids are unbelievable. Always up to something and never listening to anyone. In my day..., she reminisced to herself. Hearing the noise level jump another notch, her voice was quiet when, again, she requested the kids get settled. Still, nobody moved.

"Alright. Alright. Settle down everyone," she called. As she tried to raise the volume, her vocal chords cracked under years of strain from trying to control unrelenting classes. Most of the students heard the squeak in her tone and immediately the group sensed the lady's weakness and lack of control.

Clay scanned the room for Jason. He was nowhere to be found. Dallas was there though. As was Leon, sitting slouched over in his chair like he was half drunk. *Hmm... He probably is drunk. Or stoned.* Thankfully, Jason must have figured out it was presentation day and decided to skip this period.

If I don't do something, this is about to get serious, Clay thought. *I guess I owe Mr. Kent one.* He let out an audible sigh. *Here goes nothing.* Clay pushed his chair back and walked between the tables to Mr. Cooper's desk. He looked over at the frail, white-haired lady and said,

"I think that's supposed to be our assignment. Do you want me to hand it out?"

"Yes, please. Thank you young man," she said in return, figuring at least there was still one child in the school with any sort of values.

"It's no prob," he replied. Clay grabbed the stack of papers off the corner of the desk and began to hand them out to the other kids in the room. Some of the main trouble makers were reluctant to take a copy.

Clay was quick to think on his feet, "Hey guys, we've gotta do this. Apparently it's all gonna be on a test next day." It was a cold lie, but it seemed to do the trick and the students took a copy and began to find their way back to their desks.

As the room quieted down, Clay explained to the others in his class that Mr. Cooper was in a meeting in the main building and had asked him to help the sub get them started with the assignment and the following presentations so they wouldn't run out of precious time covering material during the year.

The old lady didn't seem to mind his help gaining their attention and his peers were just happy that Mr. Cooper wouldn't be there to see the brutality of their assignments.

Leon, on the other hand, yelled out "teacher's pet!" but, with Jason out of the room, the comment was left hanging in the air.

They spent the first twenty minutes on the worksheet and then, one by one, the kids stood and presented on various issues such as teen suicide, binge drinking and cheating in school. Nobody came to the front and nobody stood up. They were going to make it as easy on themselves as possible by simply reading from their sheets while seated at their desks.

Clay pretended not to pay attention to their work and doodled a few pictures in his binder, but he was listening attentively;

especially to the one about teen suicide which seemed to speak to him.

The substitute sat at Mr. Cooper's desk jotting down a few comments about each of the largely plagiarized presentations on the grade sheets she had been left. The only other project Clay openly paid attention to and watched intently was Dallas'. It wasn't very good either, but he listened to her speak about teenage depression and he knew she wasn't simply just presenting a topic she had been assigned, but that she was speaking from the heart.

Clay, still stirred up inside after the initial suicide speech, felt a somber connection to this girl who he could see also desperately needed some help.

As the final few minutes of the period ticked away, the old woman filling in as a teacher realized that there wouldn't be enough time for everyone to present. With Jason skipping class, his was obviously missed, but due to a lack of time, so was Clay's.

When the bell forced everyone out of the room like cattle, Clay stayed behind for a moment to help the lady push in the chairs and pick up the scraps of garbage left behind. Clay handed the woman a printed copy of his assignment and she put it, along with grade sheets and notes she had taken, on the filing cabinet next to Mr. Cooper's desk where they'd be found upon his return.

Clay felt some degree of confidence after leaving the class. It was all stripped away when he made it to the gymnasium for physical education and was greeted with calls of teacher's pet from Mark and Jason. It hadn't taken Leon long to spread the word.

Chapter IX-

A few days later, while Clay was meeting with Kent in his office, a new teacher, who was there to replace someone on stress leave, quickly popped in to introduce herself. As usual, Mr. Kent greeted her in his standard way. He always put on a fake accent and greeted new people by saying "Mr. Kent, from Oxford." And he said Oxford in a snooty, nose turned up fashion.

This had always bothered Clay. He had known for some time now that Mr. Kent had only lived in the city of Oxford, UK and had never really attended the university there as either a student nor worked there as a professor. Apparently, rumors around the student body had it that he worked as a shipper/receiver manager at Oxford University Press for a stint; a mere three years at that. But nobody ever seemed to ask for clarification and he seemed to enjoy misleading them. He could tell from the look on the new teacher's face as she left the office that she was impressed when he threw in the Oxford line with his deep vocals.

I guess his shitty accent was enough to fool these country folk, Clay thought to himself.

As their conversation came to a close, Mr. Kent brought up the fact that Clay liked to sit near the counters in the back of Mr. Cooper's room and then asked if he could take a microscope and box of supplies and put them on the counters in that room for him. Clay reluctantly agreed, not realizing how much stuff there was to carry.

Clay walked into the Annex class carrying the lab equipment that Mr. Kent had asked him to take. There was so much stuff and he had insisted Clay carry the microscope in such a way that it made it impossible to carry everything in one trip. On his second trip into the classroom, he realised that his next course, health, had already started and that his chores had made him a few minutes late. Another substitute teacher Clay had seen a few times in passing in the hallway was covering the course and Mr. Cooper was away for personal reasons again.

I guess he ended up needing another 'sick day' after all, Clay figured. *Maybe now he's just another teacher on stress leave?*

This substitute, an overbearing blond in her mid-twenties with a set of thick framed glasses and a God complex, was just starting to read the beginnings of a brief note left by Mr. Cooper on the attendance sheet regarding Clay and how he liked to hide in the rear of the class. She looked up through her opaque lenses and made a snide remark about Clay arriving late

"It's about time young man. You're quite late you realize."

His classmates snickered. As he put the microscope down on the lab bench at the back of the room, the teacher, now distracted from the note she had started reading, mentioned the class had a presentation and then a film to watch.

Of course, another movie. What a complete waste of time. Clay found a seat in one of the vacant desks near the lab bench where he hoped he could tune out during the film. Then the teacher caught him by surprise.

"Young man."

Clay looked in her general direction.

"Young man. You need to come to the front to do your presentation on cyber bullying that was assigned last week. You'll need to hurry up and get it started immediately. It's just you and Jason that are left to do your presentations. There isn't a moment to spare wasting time. We need to get the class started." She went on, "We only have time for one presentation today and Jason has already requested to go next class. So that means you are up."

The whole thing caught Clay off guard and with all this 'being late' bullshit he could feel his palms and temples start to sweat as his face grew flushed. The windows in the classroom were opened along the back wall and Clay could smell what smelled like smoke from forest fires wafting in. He too was getting hot.

Clay grumbled a bit too loudly, "Why can't I go next class too?"

The substitute overheard him. "Because you were late for class," she scolded, fed up with back talk. "Perhaps you're just worried because you haven't done your homework?"

Clay gnawed at the inside corners of his cheek with his teeth.

"Mr. Cooper had left a note mentioning that you do nothing in class anyway." The lady waved the attendance sheet with the note on it, forgetting that she had been interrupted while reading it when Clay arrived late to class holding the microscope.

It seemed unlikely, but this may have been true; after all, he hadn't seen the note in question. Clay tried not to get noticed in health class because Jason was in this course with him. That's why he always chose a seat toward the rear lab benches. But he did always listen intently even though he rarely wrote anything down. That's because many of the teachers at Pine Creek treated their students like they were two-year-olds and spoon fed them everything. Clay secretly wished the teachers would push him to work in their classes. As much as a snooty Oxford fraud that Mr. Kent was, he was the only one who actually pushed him to do better. If he just listened in health class, he didn't have to do anything else to get 100%, which is approximately what his mark was on any given day.

Clay sat down and began fumbling to find the papers with his report on them in his binder. Still stressed out and feeling everyone in the class with their eyes on him, he felt even more flushed. Flipping the pages frantically, he was unable to find his assignment. He was overheating and beginning to sweat profusely; beads of moisture now noticeable on his forehead.

"Hurry up and come to the front!" she snarled becoming ever more impatient.

"Why? Everyone else just read theirs from their desks." Clay fired back.

"Because I told you to! Now get up here and make something up if you were too lazy to do your homework. Besides," she pushed her glasses high up along the bridge of her nose to get a better look at him, "how would you know how they presented if you're always at the back and not paying attention," she barked with a stern tone.

Clay was smoking hot now. "I know because I helped to teach the freaking class that day with an idiotic substitute like you while Mr. Cooper was away having another 'bullshit sick day'!"

That was it. She had had enough. Her lips and eyebrows pinched and wrinkled as if a string drew them together from the middle of her face.

"GET OUT!" Her words stole the air from the room as she yelled for Clay to leave and head to the office.

As Clay headed storming towards the door at the front of the room, it donned on him as to why he couldn't find his papers- He had been left to be the last one to present the previous day and he had given the other substitute the hard copy of his work when helping to tidy the room after class. The elder woman had left the report on Mr. Cooper's desk with a note about how there wasn't enough time for Clay to have his turn. That's why it wasn't in his binder. Clay slammed the door to the classroom behind himself, just as the substitute read the remainder of the note on the attendance sheet.

CLAY LIKES TO HIDE NEAR THE LAB BENCHES AT THE BACK AND RARELY GETS INVOLVED IN CLASS DISCUSSIONS.

HE SELDOM SHOWS IT DURING CLASS, BUT HIS WORK IS OFTEN SUPERIOR IN QUALITY. PLEASE TAKE IT EASY ON HIM. HE'S THE TOP STUDENT IN THE CLASS AND CAN BE A BIG HELP IF NEEDED.

PS. The previous sub mentioned she left the paper for his presentation on the filing cabinet if he feels like presenting today.

MR. COOPER

She turned to the filing cabinet and saw Clay's paper sitting there on the top of the stack of the class' work. As the other students were settling down after the chaos that had just ensued, she skimmed the first of many pages. Yes, it looked perfect. Resentfully, she marked a big checkmark at the top and tossed it aside.

Chapter X-

The ordeal in the classroom was enough to get the attention of one, Dallas Hilton. Clay never did go to the principal's office and the substitute never did follow up on it. Perhaps she just realized what a bitch she had been and was hoping that Clay would stay true to his persona of being someone unlikely to say anything.

The young man spent the remainder of the period reading a text and cooling down in the upper Annex hallway. After lunch, Clay had settled down enough that he was able to go to his next class. It was a cooking class. A no brainer for most, but for Clay it meant he always had to try and figure out a way to not get paired up with certain individuals; namely Jason, Nathan, and Leon.

Today, he was paired up with Haryato, the Japanese exchange student who spoke next to no English. Haryato was another rogue student when it came to school social dynamics. Again, not by choice. By partnering with Haryato, Clay realized he wasn't going to negatively impact his own status; though he certainly wasn't going to bolster it either.

While working on making a mushroom quiche with his Japanese sidekick, Clay noticed that Dallas Hilton couldn't keep her eyes off of him as she retrieved some ingredients from across the room. Dallas had a name that sounded as if her parents were staying in a hotel on vacation when she was conceived. Unlikely, but he wouldn't put it past them. Apparently names were tough to come up with in Pine Creek. Take Jason's cronies for example: William, Billy, Nathan, Leon and Mark. Billy's real name was William too, but the teachers had long ago differentiated between the two jackasses with the spark of original thought by dubbing him Billy instead. Might as well have just left their names the same. They were asshole clones of each other anyway. They were all the same and they all dressed in typical redneck attire. Dressing up for them meant they would put on their 'nice jeans'. Some would go so far as telling their moms to wash them first.

"Pretty bad ass what you did in there." Dallas said to Clay from overtop of the back-to-back stoves separating Clay and Haryato from Dallas and her cooking partner.

"In where?" Clay responded.

"In Mr. Cooper's room- With that sub. Pretty cool the way you just told her off."

That wasn't exactly how it had gone down, but he was willing to roll with it. He was nervous talking to her. He had never really spoken to a girl before he had said "Hi" to Dallas that day in the stairwell. This was different. This was a full on conversation and he hadn't been the one to initiate it. Speaking to anyone at school was novel to him. Speaking to a girl would do nothing but help his image.

"Yeah, I guess. Aren't you Jason's girlfriend or something?"

"No. I got together with him once at a party and he thinks we are together. In case you hadn't noticed, Jason isn't the best thing to look at."

He had noticed.

"I only got together with him because I was high and because one day he might be playing professional hockey in the NHL. But I'm not really interested in him. His ear kinda grosses me out."

Clay shocked with her honesty, stood there listening attentively.

"So what's your deal anyway?" she continued. "Last year, you were about to drop out and now you're, like, acing everything."

Clay had never really considered dropping out; though he had considered suicide as an option of escape more than once. He wondered how she knew so much about him. "Just trying to get good grades so I can get outta here."

"Where? Pine Creek Community High?"

"No. Pine Creek. The town."

"Where do you wanna go to?"

"Anywhere but here. As far away from this dump as possible."

"Me too," Dallas said.

This was unexpected for Clay.

"You should go to Stonebridge. This school really doesn't suit you but you'd like that place. It's where all the nerdy kids go."

"How do you know?" Clay asked, while Haryato busily whisked some eggs in a large bowl oblivious to the conversation right beside him.

"I went there for a while."

Clay was stunned by her comment, but he stood there with a poker face refusing to show his often guarded emotions.

"Hey, do you wanna hang out after school?" she continued.

"Uhm…Okay," he said, wanting to hear more about what she knew of him and Stonebridge.

"Meet me behind the Annex building after school."

"Okay."

Dallas Hilton spun around so that her hair whipped out from her head. Clay could smell it. It smelled of fruit or berries or some girlish shampoo he thought. Then he began to wonder if this was some kind of setup and if Jason and Dallas were actually still together. *Maybe they are planning on jumping me after school?* He and Dallas didn't get a chance to speak for the duration of the class, but he couldn't stop thinking about her.

The thought of a setup ran through Clay's mind all afternoon. It was just too strange for her to start chatting him up like that. He could think of nothing else during his afternoon classes. Still, he wanted to go meet her. He wanted very much for it to be real. For her to actually want to hang out with him. When the final bell rang in the hallways, he headed to his locker in the Annex. He had to go there anyway and perhaps he would see them setting up for their big attack. Then he could run before they would ever spot him.

Clay spent all of thirty seconds at his locker before closing it and making for the door. He swung the door open and jumped down the steps missing half of them on his way. Turning the corner of the building and heading for the cover of the trees that branch out into the forest, he saw her.

"There you are," Dallas called. "I was beginning to think you stood me up."

He stopped dead in his tracks. Looking back and forth, scanning for anyone ready to jump him, he saw Jason.

And Mark.

And Billy and William.

They were all headed toward the buses. None of them seemed focused on him. In fact, they hadn't even been looking his way. He realized Dallas was sincere when she had asked to hang out. Clay walked over to her dropping his guard enough that he forgot about the possibility of an attack and fixated on her hair blowing in the gentle breeze. She grabbed his hand and said, "Let's go."

The two teens headed off into the forest taking the shortcut back to Clay's neighbourhood.

"We can go to my favourite place by the creek for a while if you want?" she said.

"Okay."

The two walked in silence through the trees. It was fairly shaded under the dark green cover of the branches and the forest floor was littered with pine needles making the ground soft. They came to a small clearing where the forest opened up to the creek. There were charred remains of a large campfire and a few empty beer cans and hard alcohol bottles lying scattered in the brush.

"Is this it?" He asked hoping she'd say no. It was the first time he'd been to this spot; although he'd heard about it while eavesdropping on other kids' stories in class.

"Na, that's where everyone parties. I like to go down here to get away from everyone sometimes." She waved her hand to gesture toward a smaller path leading along the small cobbles at edge of the creek. They walked for a few more minutes with just the sound of the water gently flowing beside them.

"Here it is."

Immediately he could see the appeal of the place. It was secluded; shady and quiet. The riffling of the creek was barely audible. There was simply creaking of the old trees as they swung from side to side in the breeze high above the forest around them. He could feel they were alone and he felt close to her.

"Should we sit down?" Clay asked.

"Sure," she said as she guided him by the hand to a large log that had the bark skinned off it long ago. She lowered herself onto the log and Clay moved over beside her.

As he put his hand on the log to brace himself while he sat down, he felt something beneath the softness of his palm. Lifting his hand from the tree trunk, he saw a heart carved into the wood. Within the heart were the initials DH +   . Dallas had left the mark carved in the trunk one day years ago when she had run into the forest after having a fight with her father when he read her diary.

She realized then, that her diary had kept too many secrets. She had always worried someone would find it and sift through the pages reading the truthfulness she had poured through the ink in between the lines of the pages. Her lack of thought for repercussions haunted her after her father found the book in her room and read the private confessions she had never dreamed would be read by any other. Often the truth in the words about her parents, teachers, friends, and boys screamed too loudly for her to continue writing. Those were the times she would cut herself. She didn't want anyone else to hear. But her father had just read a section Dallas had written about her encounters with a few of the boys at school. He charged into the room where she sat watching television and began to berate her about what he called 'whorish behaviors.' It was then that she had run to the forest crying; eventually stumbling upon this old log as a resting place away from the shame.

Clay stared at the slices etched into the wood and realized they had been carved at some point by Dallas and that she had left a spot to be filled in at a later time. He said nothing as he sat down.

Dallas began to speak just as he began to get insecure about the silence. "My dad was a millwright at a local sawmill. We had money once."

"Really?" he questioned not sure how he should respond.

"Yeah, it was a bit tight, but my family had enough money to send me to Stonebridge Academy for elementary school." She continued speaking about when production in the mills slowed due to the softwood lumber dispute with the big American companies.

Clay, caught up staring at her, was having a hard time following.

"My dad lost his job and we couldn't afford for me to stay at the school. Then my parents ended up being forced to sell our old place and we downsized to the trailer at the park across town.

Clay knew a lot of kids that lived in trailers, but this experience would have been something totally knew and inauspicious for Dallas. She was forced to transfer to Pine Creek Community High School and, as catty as teenage girls are, her friends from Stonebridge had dropped her the day she left. Dallas Hilton was human. And she too had been hurt. Clay sympathised with her as she spoke.

"I'm getting out of here too," she said. "One way or another, I'm getting out of here." She was stone cold as she spoke the words. She paused and breathed deeply a few times clearing her thoughts. Then she began to shuffle herself off of the log and kneel down on the forest floor in front of Clay. He started to get up but she pushed him back onto the log. Dallas took the button of his jeans in her hand and slowly twisted at it until it popped open. The zipper came down with ease. Clay was motionless with the exception of his heart which pounded wildly in his chest. She held him in her hands and then began to take him into her mouth.

Clay breathed deeply as the reality of the situation struck him hard. He liked this girl. He had never even kissed this girl. Until today, he had never really spoken to this girl. Clay felt uneasy and lifted her gently by the shoulders.

"What's wrong?" she said.

"I'm not ready for all of this right now."

Dallas climbed back onto the log.

"I like you and all, but I've never ever kissed you." While his nerves made him unsure what to look at, he found himself looking down at her hands.

Dallas turned to Clay and looked him over, finally resting her eyes on his. He could tell she was very embarrassed and slightly confused. She leaned in and kissed him determinedly and then got off and sped away through the forest. Clay knew she did not want to be followed and he stayed there for quite some time before heading home.

Chapter XI-

The two teens spent vast amounts of time together in the weeks ahead; most of it either down near the creek or at Clay's house. It took them a while to notice, but Mr. and Mrs. Morris were unexpectedly pleased with the fact that Clay had been bringing a girl over to the house now and then, but they weren't sure what to expect from this young lady who seemed a bit rough around the edges with her smoky dark eye make-up and hair constantly hiding the majority her face. Clay's parents said little more than the occasional "Hello. How are you?" to Dallas and they intentionally kept their distance to give the teens their space. Clay figured they hadn't really noticed her either.

During the many hours they spent hanging out, neither Clay nor Dallas had the courage to bring up the awkward moment in the forest; however, they did open up and speak about many other personal topics.

Clay had shared memories about his brother and his grandiose dreams about leaving town on a scholarship. Dallas, a bit more cautious, shared stories of her childhood, her wanting to be accepted, and her goals of one day getting away from the bindings of her hometown.

They felt they had some common bonds and became very comfortable spending time with each other outside of school. Clay treated Dallas with a level of respect she was unfamiliar with. It had won her over completely, yet it wasn't completely reciprocated.

The time spent together in school had increased Clay's 'cool factor' enough that the majority of students in his grade, aside from Jason and his friends, had stopped picking on him and now merely ignored him. On the other hand, Dallas, who was already highly self-conscious, began to secretively worry about what being seen with Clay was doing to her image. She managed to keep a bit of distance between them while at school. Her avoidance was noted by Clay, but given that this was his first experience with a girlfriend, he never assumed anything was out of the ordinary and the space was enough for him to stay on top of his classwork.

So, things went well between Clay and Dallas late into spring. Clay continued to steamroll his way through his classes and Mr. Kent was proud of his work thus far. Clay would spend time with Dallas regularly after school; often in the forest down near the river where the warmth of the pending summer breeze seemed to bring with it calmness as it flowed through the branches surrounding them in their quiet space. There, near Pine Creek, both the flowers and their relationship seemed to be blossoming.

In school, he stayed clear of trouble the best that he could. There were a few instances of verbal abuse from either Jason or his friends; especially when they would see the Dallas and him together, but those too looked as if they were decreasing in regularity. Mr. Kent, who had had a few interesting conversations with Clay's parents about the possibility of him switching schools, began securing the transfer papers for Clay in agreement with their plan and Clay appeared to be well on his way to earning that scholarship to Stonebridge.

On the other hand, Jason was becoming too preoccupied to care much for taunting Clay and Dallas. He had been hard at work on the ice rink breaking scoring records for his team in the latter part of the season. An athletic scholarship to a big university was well within his grasp as long as he could keep his marks above passing. This menial task was proving to be quite daunting for him, and at the end of the spring term, he had been placed on academic probation. This meant he either significantly improved his marks across the board, or he was unlikely to graduate. No graduation meant no athletic scholarship. It was getting down to the final minutes in the third period for Jason. So he devised a plan.

At first, the cheating started out by taking place through fairly simple means. He would write notes on his binders which would then be strategically placed on either the floor or the edge of his desk where he could view them as needed during quizzes and tests. This technique was a bit risky at times if teachers would stroll through the rows of desks during the assessments.

Next, he branched out a little and began bringing in cheat sheets; all the while, his marks continued to improve and his teachers were starting to celebrate his achievements with a bit more vigour each and every time he got another score back. He truly had them duped. The accessing and hiding of the sheets during tests and quizzes often brought undesired attention to him and he decided to hide things a little more secretively.

The next stage in his dynamic cheating plan was to write extremely tiny notes on thin strips of blank paper. Rather than entire sets of notes, now they were more like cue words or the actual answers he had been given by one of his friends who had already taken the test in a previous period. The papers were then inserted directly into the clear plastic tubes of your run-of-the-mill standard inexpensive school pens. The skinny tube of ink from within the pen lied underneath the strip of notepaper so that Jason could see the notes through the clear plastic pen walls while continuing to write. No looking around was needed. To his teachers, he would appear like he was writing intently during the quizzes. The clear plastic body of the pens actually helped to magnify the white paper strips of notes within and, should a teacher walk past, he would merely roll the pen over in his hand so that the ink sat on top of the paper slip concealing it completely. He and his friends had a lot of success with this method and even though virtually every student in the school knew what was going on, the teaching faculty was acting as if they were oblivious to his antics.

When Jason eventually pulled his marks high enough into a range that was becoming more questionable by all involved, alarms bells started going off for his instructors. Here was a child who, now at the end of grade eleven, had been bombing every single class for years. He obviously had some significant holes in his understanding of concepts and the weaknesses were often exposed when he was called upon in class discussions.

Teachers began to wonder if a student who was unable to grasp things in class was actually able to score as high as he was on his summative tests. It seemed very unlikely and they began watching him like a hawk. Jason was becoming more and more resentful of the fact that Clay had simultaneously been making basically the exact same academic turn around and had received nothing but support from his teachers, while through their intense unspoken scrutiny, he was being accused of cheating, even if they weren't really saying it to his face and would have been justified in doing so if they had. He was not one to know when to give up and he worked every angle when it came to finding new ways to beat the system.

Toward the end of the final term in their grade eleven year, as June approached, both Jason Blithe and Clay Morris knew the importance of having strong performances on their final exams. For Clay, it would send him on his way to Stonebrige Academy; one step closer to getting out of this town.

Jason, however, was a step ahead. For him, keeping himself in good academic stead for another year or so would solidify forthcoming scholarship offers to a few big schools after graduation, one of which was Michigan, who had hoped he could continue to pull through his academic hardships and perform for them as well as his brother had in years past. They were banking on him being as good, if not better, than his brother, Chris, had been. Jason would be getting out of town even earlier than Clay, if he could carry on performing both on and off the ice.

Clay spent hours studying for each of his finals. He alternated between studying in his bedroom and at Pine Creek Public Library. The school library was no place to get work done.

When exam week came, he knew he was prepared. Jason too was primed. He and William were desperate to get hold of the tests before hand. They had contracted out the help of a former peer at Pine Creek Community High School who had since moved on to Stonebridge last year himself.

Myles Carter had moved to Pine Creek from New York City a couple of years ago. His parents were wealthy owners of a hotel chain that was starting construction of a new hotel in the west side of town. Because they had arrived in Pine Creek in October, they were a little too late getting Myles signed up for courses at Stonebridge and were forced to put him on a waiting list while he would attend classes at the local public high school in the meantime. With his hard sounding New York accent, people like Jason and his crew were immediately drawn to Myles. They befriended him for a while but soon lost interest when they realized he was not the street-wise gangster they were hoping he might be.

Instead, Myles was a bright young man, of slight build, who played the part of the rugged New Yorker while at Pine Creek School, but immediately transformed into his current persona of trendy hipster while at Stonebridge. He hadn't cut all ties with Jason or his buddies and actually would hang out from time to time on the weekends with Leon and William. It was this relationship that allowed Jason to nearly ace his final exams.

He and his friends would wait for their teachers to photocopy the finals, and then find ways to steal them. In one circumstance, Billy and William had actually distracted their mathematics teacher, Miss Johnson, in the photocopy room with stories of hockey fights while Jason had snuck in a mere five feet behind them as they spoke to her to steal a warm copy of the final exam right off the printer. They were able to acquire all but two of their finals, one of which was health and no university would care about that mark anyway.

Myles would receive a payment of twenty dollars for every test that he would write for them beforehand. The crew would each make a copy of the answers for themselves and would study them until they had memorized the responses in entirety. Then, confidently and casually, they would head into the exam rooms, write the tests, and await the news of their fantastic results. Though some were skeptical, the teachers and administrators were none the wiser.

Chapter XII-

The final graduation assembly of the school year was held in the Pine Creek Community High School gymnasium on a humid and stuffy afternoon in late June. It was suffocating in the gym as students crowded onto the old bleachers; teachers stationed in chairs on the gym floor in front of them careful to not to have their backs toward the crowd. The administration was poised at the front, ready to hand out rolled diplomas tied with blue ribbons to those few seniors who had graduated and letters of accomplishment with information about summer school to those who had not.

The students not in the graduating class and a smattering of parents were also packed into the bleachers to provide an audience for those being celebrated. Far from being entertained, they fanned themselves with their hands in attempt to keep themselves awake and cool.

Clay was called to the front by Mr. Kent and Ms Thompson to receive news of his strong performance in grade eleven and the offer of his full tuition scholarship to Stonebridge Academy for his senior year starting in the fall. Jason was particularly taken aback by this announcement as he had not seen it coming and had been enjoying the thought of tormenting Clay for another twelve months. Dallas remained stone-faced when she heard the news, realizing she too was to be left behind by her boyfriend.

Mr. Kent received a lukewarm ovation from the student body and faculty for his retirement announcement. Surprisingly, most of the teachers and some of the students were able to hide their giggles and snickers when he claimed he was off to Oxford over the summer.

Jason, Billy, and Mark each took turns mocking and cat calling the senior students strutting across the gym floor to receive their diplomas. William and Leon pondered the idea of what it might be like to swagger across the stage next June to receive their respective letters of accomplishment, which they would promptly toss in the trash upon leaving the gymnasium at the end of the ceremony. Leon joked that if, and when, he ever received a diploma, he'd burn it on stage in front of the school principal.

Chapter XIII-

After the notification of his scholarship, Clay was invited by Mr. Isaacs, the Principal at Stonebridge Academy to come for a visit of the facilities. Clay spent one of the late days of June touring the school with Mr. Isaacs, an imposing behemoth of a man who commanded the attention of everyone they passed in the hallways. Though he was awestruck by its splendor and excited about the opportunity to attend, he tried not to bring up the subject around Dallas when he saw that she became withdrawn each time the topic arose.

Clay and Dallas spent a lot of time together over the summer. They spent much of it sharing stories, while hanging out in either the town library, Clay's bedroom, or down by the river in the woodlands. The two of them knowing that they had similar hopes and dreams but two very distinctive paths to follow. Dallas seemed to be becoming less restrained around him and he too, was able to let his guard down and talk to her without worrying about the consequence of how he might be judged. Dallas hadn't had an incident of cutting in quite some time. She often found herself reassessing her own worth now that she had a boyfriend who actually cared about her well-being.

Clay's relationship with his parents hadn't changed much, but they were minutely excited to hear about him being accepted into Stonebridge on a full ride. Clay hadn't spent a lot of time at home over the summer, and thus, hadn't personally done a great deal to strengthen his family ties either.

A week or so before the summer holiday was to come to an end, Clay's parents decided they would go away for the weekend. They left on a Friday after his father had finished work. Clay was to stay behind and watch the house. They had no pets and few plants; certainly none that would require regular watering.

Clay figured that their choosing to get away meant they likely just needed to be away from him. Feeling a bit lonely, he had texted Dallas a couple of times the night before and again in the morning, but she had not yet responded. With his parents gone and Dallas preoccupied with something at home, Clay, a bit concerned that she had not responded, decided to head off to walk around his new school for something to do to kill time.

The initial tour from Mr. Isaacs was brief and he didn't really have a feel for the school yet. He wanted to get acquainted with the new facility early so that he wouldn't end up looking like a fool lost in the hallways on the first day of school. He walked to the entrance of the grand building, gated and closed for the summer. The double iron gate was tall, roughly seven feet high, with intricate swirls and loops, two of which formed the capitalized letters S and A. It was a bold declaration stating that 'if you aren't part of this particular school community, don't bother coming to visit.'

Clay looked to make sure there were no hidden cameras before hopping over the gate; the drop on the other side seemed higher than he had expected. He walked up the circular road surrounding a large fountain preceding the stairs to the front door. The fountain, an over-sized, circular marble pool about two feet deep, was off for now, but would spray clear water throughout the fall and spring months. The front door was solid wood, with panels to improve its elegance. It fit in well with the natural stone walls and dark cherry walnut stained trim. The stone was not just a façade; the walls were solid rock, as they should be. A large school crest made out of marble was positioned centrally above the doors, locking the fortress tight. Words in Latin ran the length of a stone banner just below the crest. He had never learned any Latin at Pine Creek Community High School, but he felt assured the words said something purveying meaning.

Clay turned down the wide stairs over toward the fountain and sat on the low wall holding in the water of the pool. He threw a coin in and watched the ripples flow out across the water, wishing he could be anywhere but in his current town. He tossed another, wishing he had some way of getting even with Jason for all that he had done to him, and then a final coin, wishing Jason was actually dead.

Dallas was in his thoughts too. He wasn't sure what to wish about her yet. Perhaps that was for the best; he was all out of coins. *Where was she anyway?* He hadn't seen her all day and she still wasn't answering his texts from last night. Clay stood up and took his time walking home from the school, trying to figure out just how long it would take him to make the trip each day.

As soon as he got home, he had a real bout of loneliness. Months had passed since he had felt this way. The evening dragged on and Clay took to reading one of the novels Mr. Kent had given him to pass the time until he would be tired enough to drift off to sleep.

When Dallas' text to his cell phone interrupted, he was thrilled. Nobody else ever called him personally and there was no legitimate reason he should even have a cell phone, but his parents thought he could make use of Mr. Morris's old phone and had agreed for him to keep it in case of emergencies.

He invited Dallas over making sure to casually slip the fact that his parents were gone into the conversation. She arrived at his porch just before ten o'clock and wrapped on the screen door. Clay hustled to answer the door, opening it to find her standing there in the summer twilight wearing a kilt and blouse. The Hilton's had established no curfews for Dallas and she was free to stay out as late as she wanted any night of the week without them ever taking the care to wonder where she was or what she was up to.

"What's this all about?" Clay admired her in the kilt knowing it was traditionally worn as part of the Stonebridge uniform by girls who went there.

While staring at her legs and imagining what was hidden under the plaid grey and royal blue kilt, he noticed several marks on her skin that had been hidden up until this point. There were etchings- lines carved and forming thin raised scars on her inner thighs. He chose to ignore them for the moment realizing now was not the time to ask about them.

"What? My outfit? I figured I'd wear this outfit one more time to prove that I actually did go to Stonebridge once."

Clay now realized why her skirt was so short- it was the one she wore years ago. He was not about to complain.

"I just don't want you getting hooked on those private school girls when you're there and forgetting about me. I want you to take me with you when you escape this town."

Clay led her by the hand inside and shut the door. The two went up to Clay's room where she turned on some music on his stereo and tossed her handbag on the nightstand. Before lying down, he had taken off his jeans and she, her kilt, taking a moment to unfasten the sturdy kilt pin that had held it together and put it on the dresser beside the bed.

The two of them crawled under the heavy blankets and pillows together, drawing closer in his bed. The lights were off, but for the first while, the room was dimly lit by the last breaths of daylight shining through the curtains. They held each other and chatted about the heat of the day and the small, bleakness of the town and how little it had to offer. By about eleven, the room was incredibly dark and they had listened to both sides of the record she had playing.

Dallas Hilton rolled towards Clay and kissed him on the neck. He kissed her back, this time on the lips. He could taste the berry flavour of her lip gloss. He tried to pull his head away to look at her but she grabbed him by the back of the head and held his lips against hers. They kissed more intently; their tongues twisting against each other's. Dallas slipped under the blanket, removed Clay's boxers and took him in her mouth. He stretched out across the bed and she took her time with him before climbing over to the nightstand and reaching for a condom from inside her bag. She went back below the covers and skillfully placed it on him.

Clay pulled the blanket down to see her. As she raised her head he asked if she could take off her shirt. Dallas sat up straddling his waist and slowly unbuttoned the blouse. With one arm she held her shirt while she used her other to unhook her bra and slip it off. She reached both arms out from her sides each holding an element of clothing that had once covered her beautiful body. She paused for a moment before letting them fall to the floor.

Clay took a deep breath while he stared at the silhouette that was the outline of her body. The two embraced and made love quietly under the cover of the darkness. It was Clay's first experience and it was everything he had dreamt it would be.

They slept there for a couple of hours together. Clay awoke to find Dallas standing in the light of a small book lamp, wearing the kilt and doing up the last couple of buttons on her shirt. She reached for the pin on the dresser. Once again, Clay noticed the scars on her legs. This time he asked.

"What happened to your legs?"

Dallas immediately pulled the kilt lower and squeezed her thighs together trying to conceal the marks.

"I used to do it when I was young and stressed about stuff. Nobody has seen them before. Please don't tell anyone. I had to see Ms Thompson for a while to chat about other ways to deal with stress."

"You cut yourself?" Clay asked in a hushed, confused voice.

Guys just don't understand. "Don't worry about it. I'm fine. It was just something I did as a dumb kid." She was right. Clay wouldn't understand. Not this time. She had her own set of issues. *Maybe that's why we are so good together?* he thought.

"Is that what you were doing in the staircase the first time I saw you?" Clay asked hoping the subject had changed just enough to avoid the cutting issue she seemed so sensitive about.

"What?"

"Going to see Ms Thompson, I mean. I saw you in the staircase when I had to go write some tests up there."

"Yeah. I was waiting to have my meeting with Ms Thompson. I don't need to chat with her anymore. She just likes me to check in with her every few months. I've had to do it for years. She's cool though. Anyway, I don't want to talk about this anymore. Just give me some space."

Clay could tell she wasn't angry; that she just needed some breathing room. Besides, he was preoccupied with the thought that she must have remembered the first time they had crossed paths in the stairs too. Needing space was something Clay understood well. *Maybe that's why we're so good together?* he thought again.

"Here. A way to remember this night." She held out her opened hand revealing the kilt pin and tossed it to him on the bed. It landed on the blanket near his knees. "I have to go home." Dallas walked out of the room and down the stairs.

Clay admired the sharpness of the pin as he held it in his hand. He placed it on his dresser and flopped back down on the bed, quickly drifting off to sleep.

Chapter XIV-

On the last Saturday afternoon just before the first day of what would be his grade twelve year, while Clay was out in the yard finishing up mowing the grass at his family's home, Mark stopped by in his truck. Few high school kids from Pine Creek could afford their own vehicles and Mark's truck was nothing special- in the sense that it was an old extended cab GMC with rusted out side panels and one dented white door, while the rest of the vehicle was a navy blue.

Mark's father was a mechanic and Mark had spent many hours after school and throughout the summers apprenticing in the shop or in their family's garage. Mark's home was the type of place where car parts were strewn haphazardly across the front yard. Grass that had once gown had been replaced by grey colored silt from years of wear and misuse storing big chunks of metal parts.

Mark had earned enough money working in his dad's shop that he was able to purchase a lift kit, some large mudder tires and a snorkel exhaust system designed to keep dust and water out of the air intake and protect the engine during the time he would spend off-roading in the back country.

Mark parked the large truck on the sidewalk in front of Clay's home and shut down the engine, which was sputtering so loudly that it was drowning out the sound of the lawnmower.

Clay turned and wondered what he could possibly be doing parked at his house. He could see that Leon and Billy were sitting squished into the back seat of the cab. It was bad enough that they had bullied him last year at school, but now they had come to his home during the summer when school was out.

Clay walked across the freshly mowed lawn as Mark hopped out of the driver's side of the vehicle and walked around the front, taking care not to get caught up in the winch mounted on the front of his metallic beast.

"What do you want?" Clay asked, keeping a fair amount of distance between the two of them.

"We thought you might want to play some football," replied Mark.

"With you guys? What gives?"

"We know you're off to Stonebridge next year and we won't likely see you after that. Anyway, we really aren't that bad. Mostly we just act like jerks to you when Jason's around. We don't really mean it. Nothing against you, you know."

"Besides, we only have three guys and we need four to play anything anyway," Leon chirped as he leaned himself over the back of the front seat so that he could yell out the window.

Confusion, years of loneliness and a desperate want to be accepted by everyone drove Clay to agree to play. "Let me just put the lawnmower away and get some different shoes on. I'll be right there." He pushed the mower into the garage, leaving the bag of grass still attached. He was too excited to take it off now. He could always do that when he got home. For now, he was breaking into a very select group.

Clay jumped up the stairs in his garage and into a door that led to the landing where his runners were awaiting him. Clay kicked off the ratty old sneakers he'd been wearing to mow the lawn and quickly slipped on his runners, not wasting time tying them up before running out of the garage toward the truck.

"Hey," he said to Leon and Billy in the back seat as he stepped on the running board and climbed in the open white door.

"Hey," Leon replied. Billy was sitting behind the driver's seat; his knee bouncing up and down nervously.

Must not have had his Ritalin, Clay thought. This kid was always on edge. In school, he constantly annoyed his teachers by just getting up and strolling around the classroom at the most inappropriate times. When the school finally discussed Billy's rambunctious and distracting nature with his parents, they were quick to take him straight to their family physician and request Ritalin to calm him down. Half the time he looked like he was stoned, the other half of the time he had difficulty controlling his emotions and his body parts, which shook with the type of anticipation of a kid waiting to open presents on Christmas morning. Sitting in the back seat tapping his foot and drumming his fingers on the driver's headrest, it seemed like this moment was a situation like the latter described.

Mark climbed into the captain's chair and fired up the engine. It started with a sputter, followed by a rumble before lurching forward. Mark stomped on the gas pedal and quickly shifted through the first few gears. Clay hoped none of his neighbours would see him in the truck. Seconds later, Clay was tearing through the streets of Pine Creek riding shotgun in Mark's old pick up. He wondered what Dallas Hilton would have thought had she been around to see him hanging out with these guys.

"Where are we going to play?" Clay asked.

"At some park," Mark said. He drove for a few minutes and Clay sat in silence beginning to wonder which park they could possibly be going to as the they passed a couple of empty fields on their way towards the outskirts of town. They were just about to turn onto the highway when it happened.

"Shoot! Did you guys feel that?" Mark said in a half excited manner. "I think I just got a flat." Leon and Billy looked at each other in the back seat. Billy's knee was still shaking vigorously and Leon started laughing. Mark geared down and pulled the truck over to the shoulder on the side of the highway.

Mark opened the door to his truck and began to hop out. "Can you check your side?" He looked at Clay who looked stunned for a second and then suddenly understood that the comment was referring to him.

"Ya, I got it," Clay said. Clay pried the door open and stepped down off the running board onto the gravel.

Leon flipped the seat in front of him forward and leaned his body partially through the open door as if to look outside. Clay looked at the front tire. The thick treaded black rubber seemed to be intact. Nothing seemed to be sticking out of it.

"Check the back ones!" Billy blurted from the back seat.

Clay stepped past the open door walking along the passenger side of the vehicle towards the back of the truck. Just then, Leon grabbed the handle of the door and slammed it shut. Mark jumped into his waiting driver's seat, slamming the door behind him.

Clay looked up at them through the glass of the truck door.

Billy, unable to control himself any longer, belted out with laughter as Leon pushed the lock down on his door and Mark started up the truck. They said nothing as they drove off.

Clay, realizing all of his faults at once, stood there in the dust angry at the world. It was a long, long walk back home. Clay knew he would never again let his guard down.

Chapter XV-

Clay arrived home a number of hours later. An express package had been dropped off for him and it was left on the top front step, not on the porch. Clay picked up the thick envelope sealed shut with a half role of packing tape and opened the corner of it with his teeth as he walked through the front door to his home. This mail addressed to him was unlike any birthday or Christmas card he'd received and it would not be promptly thrown away the same afternoon. This mail was different. It was something he would keep and read in the privacy of his room.

He tore the end of the package and spit out a small piece of tape that had been caught between his teeth. As he tipped it over, a book slid into his empty hand. It was a copy of a travel book about England. Clay turned the envelope over and, in the corner, saw the sender's name and address: Kent, Oxford, UK. Clay bent the spine slightly in his hands and thumbed through the pages. A small handwritten note on a sheet of paper from a notepad flipped out.

Perhaps one day you'll come visit this place? Enjoying vacation and retirement. A lot of good universities here you know.

There was nothing more. Clay took the book upstairs to his room and shut the door. He read it cover to cover throughout the night, stopping only to fantasize about places he could go; far away, rich with history and so very different from Pine Creek.

The next morning Clay phoned Dallas to ask if she wanted to hang out. He could tell by the way she answered that something was bothering her. The two talked about how great their summer together had been going. Clay left out the part about Mark and the truck. When he finally asked if she wanted to meet down by the river, she told him she'd come by his place later that night.

Again, Dallas arrived around ten o'clock. He wasn't sure why she always showed up so late, but it made little difference to him even though tomorrow would be the first day of school. His parents weren't planning to be home until the following day. They headed up to his room and got under the covers as they had a few nights earlier.

He rubbed his hand across her lower back slipping his fingers under the waistband of her panties. Nothing. She lay perfectly still. He continued to gently slide his cautious hand over her body from the crease of her bum to her shoulders. This time she rolled onto her side facing the darkness of the room. He persisted. He ran his hand softly up the back of her thigh until it once again met the silky fabric covering the most sensuous part of her. His fingers inched close enough that he could feel her.

"I'm tired," she said. "Besides, I'm breaking up with you, Clay. Jason and I are going out. He's going to university to play hockey soon and I've always kinda liked him." There was no way anyone could have been further apart than the two of them lying there together.

I'm tired too, he thought. *Tired of pretending they would always be together. Tired of trying.* "*Tired of Dallas.*" Only that part he had said aloud. He had a problem with mumbling out his true feelings at inopportune times.

And she heard it. It surprised both of them that he said it. Neither were surprised that he meant it.

He angrily rolled out of bed and struggled to put on his jeans. The cuff got caught on his toes and he tugged hard to pull it past causing him to curse under his breath. She said nothing. He could sense she was crying now but he didn't care and he didn't wait to put on the rest of his clothes. He just scooped them up into his arms and walked out of the room and down to the kitchen.

He felt surprised again; surprised that he had no urge to look back at the stunned, fractured girl lying half naked under a blanket and some tears. A few minutes later she emerged dressed, and left the house without a word.

In an instant his adoration of this woman became wicked and foul. It was impossible for him to see it coming. The flames grew closer that night in his dreams. At one point, the smell woke him and, for a second, he worried there were forest fires nearing the town. Now the flames were close enough that he could smell ash burning in the air as he tried to sleep. The stench almost choked him as he started to slide into an uneasy, restless slumber. Growing bloodshot and weary, Clay's eyes closed for the night. Now that he was completely alone, there was nobody he could tell about the fires inside him.

The remainder of the weekend was hot and lonely for Clay. He spent much of it listening to Sam Cooke albums in his room.

Chapter XVI-

The library at Stonebridge was in stark contrast to the one at Pine Creek Community High School and he found it quickly again on the first day of school. On his tour a few months prior, this part of the school had interested him more than any other. The dark stained doors were shamelessly menacing as they reached nearly to the ceiling in the hallway; the school's crest carved deep into the rich, cherry stained wood.

The fact that the doors were made of imported South American mahogany, not a tree native to the area like pine or fir, likely pissed off the locals as well, he thought to himself. *They couldn't even sacrifice their high society ideals for the local economy when building this place. No wonder most of the people in this town hate these eco-friendly guys.*

He pushed the door handle down and swung one of the heavy slabs open. *So, this is how the other half lives.* Clay took a moment to take it in, breathing deeply as his eyes opened wide enough to let in as much of the view as possible.

The library was out of this world. It was like a throwback to some medieval library like one would expect tucked away in an old castle. *It even smells of newly printed paper*, he noted. Towering shelves of books stacked all the way up. Brass coloured ladders on rails adorned each of the side walls so that the top stacks could be accessed. And everything built with the same imported opulently stained wood. There was even a gas fireplace here with a couple of new leather chesterfields flanking its sides as they wrapped around a coffee table that must have cost a fortune. The image reminded him of a painting he had once seen of the President. He could imagine him sitting by the fire smoking a pipe and reading the newspaper. Likely what the founders of the school had in mind when they built this place.

As he walked deeper into the rows of books, each labeled with shiny brass plaques specifying their collections, he saw where a large chunk of the student body was gathered toward the back of the library. They had done a great job with the design of this part of the building. Though unearned as it may be in its new beginnings, the overall feeling of the room was that there was some degree of prestigious history here. Yet, the space was filled with all of the latest technologies.

Wirelessly capable, the students with their laptops and smart phones could check e-books in and out without the need for a librarian. In fact, there were more on-line books available to them through the school's cyber library located on its website than there were piled endlessly on the shelves here. A separate room with glass walls made a sound-proof meeting space where students and faculty could be wowed with presentations on several Smart boards and large touch screens. A bank of independent cubicles, each with various receptacles and ports for kids to plug in their personal electronics, lined one of the back walls.

Because the students at Stonebridge were so tech savvy and had the means to buy any new piece of personal electronics they wished, even the new gadgetry of this library was quickly becoming outdated. The workstations were seldom used for watching any film; instead the kids would do everything on the phones and touch sensitive pads they had glued to themselves. The workstations were quickly becoming places only used as charging stations for repowering their priceless devices.

Man, I'm glad that the kids at Pine Creek Community High School have never seen this room- There's no real likelihood that they ever would, given it's a library, Clay thought.

Clay had quickly made a few friends in the coming weeks of September. None of them he would call close friends, but at least they were people he could sit with at lunch and talk to in the hallways before and after school. Myles Carter was one of them. He had recognized Clay right away and, in an attempt to secure Clay's friendship and the secret about his embarrassing alternate street persona from his time at Pine Creek School, Myles had partnered up with Clay on the first day of school to introduce him to others and show him around. Clay would take any friendship that came along these days even if it was from some snotty rich kid with an unearned sense of entitlement.

Chapter XVII-

The Morris family had been struggling with financial woes for as long as Clay had been in high school. Finally, it came to a point where it was necessary for them to downsize to another home in their neighborhood. The move wasn't exactly too disruptive for Clay as he had never really been too attached to the house in the community he so desperately wanted to leave. He thought it might be good for his parents. Moving into a smaller house would mean all of his brother's things would finally get boxed up, and the emptiness that was his room would no longer serve as a constant reminder of Neil's absence.

For the first time since his early childhood, Clay felt happy to go to school. He was excited about the chance to meet new people each day who might be interested in their studies enough to have meaningful conversations in class. Clay had enrolled in all the A-level courses so that he could keep his options open for colleges. And now that he was inspired and no longer felt the pressures of being forced to watch over his shoulder or keep his mouth shut in class, he was able to truly be himself academically. Clay got along well with his teachers and once he figured out exactly what they were looking for in terms of quality work, he was able to provide them with it. Clay came through the front door each day at his new school. There was no Annex and no need to hide in certain hallways or staircases.

As he passed the Stonebridge front office just inside the entrance one morning, the school secretary advised Clay that a package had been sent over to Pine Creek School addressed to him, care of Ms Thompson. It seemed that because of his family's recent change of residence, the sender no longer had his permanent home address and figured Ms Thompson could track him down and pass on the mail. She had left it at the office over at Pine Creek and their office staff had left a message instructing Clay to come by after school to pick it up.

Across town, Jason continued where he had left off; strutting through the hallways as if he owned the place. Clay knew walking through the trails of the forest that separated the schools that he'd need to be quick and unnoticed as he approached Pine Creek School. He had waited as long as he could to make the trip, hoping the office would still be open and that most of the students would have left on the buses. Arriving at the office, he found the secretary unusually helpful as she began to hand him the package without any trouble.

"My, you sure have grown, young man," said the secretary eyeing Clay up and down.

His gaze dropped while he looked himself over as he panned back up from his feet to the height of the desk.

"I guess so." he agreed. Clay could tell a book was inside the bubble wrapped envelope as he took it from her outstretched palm, but he decided to wait until he was in the privacy of his room before opening it. He stuffed it inside his old forest green backpack.

Clay scurried out the door at the end of the hall by the gymnasium, along the cement walkway leading toward the old Annex, and around the corner of the building where he was caught by surprise.

William, Leon and Mark were there, the first two of them each holding a freshman. Leon had one by the wrist on his right arm. The kid's left shirt sleeve was torn and his jeans were covered in grass stains. At least this one had put up a fight. Mark held the other kid tightly around the neck in a headlock. He had never considered fighting back. Leon let go of his captive who took off around the building as fast as his legs could carry him. Mark pushed his own prey to the ground.

"Get lost kid," he threatened.

The undersized dusty kid sheepishly got up and scampered away after his friend.

"Look who has come to visit us, guys," Leon said. He pounced at Clay and grabbed him by the sleeve; the yank breaking the zipper on his green book bag tearing it open as it flipped out of his hand and onto the cement. Clay tugged sharply at his shirt and tried to shake his arm free. A button popped off the cuff and Leon held fast. Mark stepped over and punched Clay in the stomach then grabbed him by his school tie, which was still buttoned to the top of his neckline. It choked at him like thick smoke.

"Don't bother trying to fight back, Tree Hugger. And nice fucking uniform, by the way."

Clay buckled at the knee for a moment and then struggled to gain his footing and stand upright again. The three collaborators walked Clay around the side of the building to where the school playing fields were located.

A couple more freshmen who were standing there against the fence were awaiting their initiations. Clay dropped his eyes as he was led past them. His nerves had him shaking on the outside and breaking inside. Jason and Billy were standing at the top of the steep, patchy, grassy hill that gave way below to the poorly maintained running track surrounding the soccer field.

"Yes! Un-fuckin' believable," Jason cried out when he caught sight of the four of them rounding the corner toward the summit of the hill. "This is gonna be awesome."

"Look at his gay uniform," Billy commented, feeling the need to get his two cents in.

There was more that was said by the group, but Clay, resorting back to the protective measures he had developed during his previous encounters with these teens, had quickly let his mind block out the sounds of their voices to protect him from the verbal abuse.

The ground was steep enough where they stood that the physical education teachers would often make any students who showed up late for their classes run up and down 'Heart Attack Hill,' as they dubbed it, for as long as they could possibly hack it. This punishment for tardiness rarely lasted any more than a couple of minutes as weary students could handle no more.

103

When the prisoner was taken to the top of the hill, one of his guards kicked at the back of his knee dropping him to the ground. Another pushed him from his kneeling position onto his back. Mark, William and Leon jumped on his chest, sitting on top of him. The wind was expelled forcefully out of Clay's lungs and he struggled to even moan in pain as they adjusted their positions and held him tightly. Jason gripped his left ankle; Billy his right. They spun him a quarter turn so that his feet pointed down Heart Attack Hill and they began to drag.

The grass didn't seem as lush now. Every small depression and bulge in the green carpet tormented his back. The hillside seemed much longer from his current vantage point and he was waiting within the walls of his mind for the bottom to come. Pebbles ate at his shoulder blades and spine. Unable to breathe with the weight on his chest, he could not muster a cry for help.

The three freshman youngsters watching in horror near the building fled from the summit. There was nobody there to stop the descent. They eventually stopped when they reached the track at the bottom of the hill and the boys ran off laughing hysterically. Before bolting, William climbed off Clay's chest and paused for enough time to kick him once in the ribs.

Clay lied there for a minute catching his breath before stammering to his feet. As he arched his back to stand erect, he could feel the burn in the wrinkles of his skin. His back, like his shirt, had been torn like a sheet of tissue paper. The powder blue uniform dangled in ribbons for a moment before sliding off his shoulders and onto the ground. Where there were once soft patches of skin it was now red and littered with blades of grass and small stones, which had embedded themselves and been dragged through the flesh like a glacier pushes rocks on the countryside. Clay stood looking like a burn victim. He brushed debris from his elbows and realized the grass stains underneath weren't coming off of his skin. He picked at the patch of turf that was caught under his belt at the rear of his school trousers. The wear on his back paled in comparison to the wear on his soul. His heart bore more damage than his back and he had been broken.

The hill had lived up to its name. He didn't bother with picking up the remains of his shirt but climbed the hill to find the backpack he had left behind, torn but still holding the book within, before staggering home through the dimness of the trees.

Chapter XVIII-

Upon arriving home, Clay walked past his mother to the stairs leading up to his room. She was standing near the dining table, too spaced out on her anti-depression medication to notice his shirtless body or the damage that had been done to his dorsal side. The stairs creaked, as did his aching bones, while he mustered up the last of his dwindling energy pulling himself hand-over-fist up the bannister.

In his room, Clay took the book, still wrapped in packaging, out of the tattered backpack where it had been kept. He tucked it under his armpit for a moment while he examined the damage done to the zipper on the bag. The teeth had been pulled free of the zipper and it was obviously unfixable. Clay retrieved the kilt pin Dallas had given him from where it sat on his dresser and used it to pin together the two cloth sides hoping it would do the trick in repairing the damage. *Good enough*, he thought. Then he tossed the bag aside and grabbed the book from where it had been tucked under his arm. Clay noticed the sender's address once again: Oxford, UK. He smiled. The teen peeled back the extensive tape-covered opening to the envelope and slid out the book. It was *On the Road*, by Jack Kerouac, an author he'd never heard of. Clay flipped the book open to find a note from Mr. Kent.

You'll like this book, Clay. It's about a group of friends travelling across the country as written through the eyes of the narrator, Sal Paradise. His last name says it all. Give it a read.

Mr. Kent

Clay continued paging through the text. He stumbled across a line on one of the pages from the character Sal: *"The only people in life for me are the mad ones... the ones who never yawn or say a commonplace thing, but burn, burn, burn like fabulous yellow roman candles."* Clay thought of himself never saying anything too, and then the repetitive use of the term *"burn"* reminded him of his back. It hurt, stinging him with heat.

He went to the upstairs bathroom at the end of the hallway and took an aspirin out of the medicine cabinet, then stripped down and had a cool shower washing off the embarrassment with the grass and dirt. The water drizzling from the shower head couldn't seem to wash his back completely clean; each drop pounded as it hit his tenderized flesh.

Chapter XIX-

Dallas Hilton and Jason Blithe had been going steady for several weeks. If by steady, one thinks of the dreadful circumstance of one individual being utterly controlled by another. Dallas, seeing her graduating class a mere eight months from the end of their schooling, was manic in her attempt to find a way out of Pine Creek. Few kids from Pine Creek High would be applying for colleges out of town in the fall. Even fewer still would actually be accepted into college. So, the only way she could visualize her escape happening was to cling on like a piece of plastic wrap to someone like Jason who had a window of opportunity in sports. His brother had done it; at least for a little while. All she needed was a one way ticket and a place to crash for a bit until she could get her footing.

Jason's shot at the hockey big leagues was set, provided he could keep up his marks. His regime of stealing tests and having other kids do them for him was working perfectly and he fully planned on riding that train right through finals to the graduation ceremony at the end of the year. His die had been cast and he was well versed in letting it ride.

When Jay, as Dallas called him, finished school at the end of each day, he had a couple hours of free time before hockey practice. Three times per week he had two-a-days where his team was able to get regular evening ice time and throw an extra practice in before school.

These should be enough to keep someone busy, but Jason seemed to have plenty of extra time to hang out. Little of this time was spent with Dallas. He would divide his time between Mark, Billy and the gang, and her. The division was far from an even split. If she wanted time with him, it was tagging along at his side while he and his buddies caused mayhem during the school day or it was swinging by his place late at night.

Getting out after dark was not a problem for her; however, the trek to his place was hardly worth the time. One night, she arrived shortly after ten or eleven o'clock, when Jay's parents were fast asleep. He had the partially developed rec-room in the basement as his personal space. The door at the bottom of the stairs was securely locked with a punch code key pad on the door just below the handle. The lone holder of the code, Jason, secured privacy for his undertakings. Jason had played around with a lot of small locks on cabinets and storage containers as a kid and had figured out a way to pick most of them with a couple of safety pins or bent paper clips. He no longer trusted their usefulness and had spared no expense on his electronic coded lock. His parents had no access, no way to check on him, even if they did want to.

Within the bowels of his basement pad laid one large rug designed to replicate an ancient Persian boldly patterned with reds and burgundies, on top of which sat his mattress. The frame and box spring had been broken long ago in some wrestling match that had gotten out of hand. Several pillows of varied size were scattered at the head of the bed, while at the foot, piled up, were a couple of worn comforters. A few scrap pieces of carpet had been laid on the cement foundation floor creating a pathway from the main rug to one door leading to the stairs and to another heading into the en-suite bathroom. Baseboards had been put on the walls leaving gaps between them and the cement with anticipation of one day parting wall from lush carpeting. An old standing lamp, missing the lampshade, provided some light along with a single bulb hanging from the knock down ceiling; a broken chain dangling just out of reach.

The bathroom was less complete. Plumbing was in place and working but the walls remained in a time lag waiting for mudding, taping and a couple of coats of fresh paint. There weren't any working lights in the bathroom so the door was routinely left wide open so that the dim light of the bedroom could provide enough luminance to see. His parents obviously were in too much of a rush in moving him into his own space away from them to finish the renovation. He was all too willing to oblige.

As Dallas arrived at the house, she knew better than to knock or ring the buzzer. Instead, she let herself in by reaching through a hole torn in the screen door and unlocking it from the other side. The main door was never kept locked. Nobody was going to break into this house anyway. If they did, Jason and Chris, when he too used to live at home, would have had a field day injuring the would-be thief without repent.

She headed downstairs to the basement suite door having already texted Jay to let him know she was almost there so that he would anticipate her knock. He let her in and the booty call started. There was never a case of attachment or love on nights like this; rather, it was one-sided animal promiscuity in its simplest form.

She peeled her clothes off as fast as possible and climbed under the comforters, hoping he didn't get a chance to see her. Dallas hated the thought of the last time the blankets had been washed and what, or who, else had been done in the bed. Jay pulled off his jeans and underwear and commented under his breath, "You better be on the pill."

"Don't worry about it," Dallas said. *Thank god,* she thought.

Sometimes he didn't have the patience to take off his shirt or socks. Today was one of those times. He kept his ball cap on too; something she hated. Then he mounted her. Each time he had done this, it was as if he had been a prisoner serving a life sentence and ten years in, he'd been granted a conjugal visit with a Playmate. It was rushed, frantic and dull.

He was no bigger than anyone else she'd been with, but he sure thought he was. If he lasted long enough, he'd usually lean on top of her and blurt out some inappropriate remark. She waited for it unenthusiastically.

"Yeah, you can't handle me. You liked that didn't you?" he said.

Is he serious or just being sarcastic? she wondered without saying a word as he continued.

Dallas laid there like a starfish, purposefully keeping her head tucked to the right side of his head whilst he did the deed, so as not to see or come in contact with his cauliflower ear. The scarred face was bad enough, but that would be just too much for her to block out during the already painful enough session. The brim of his hat was annoyingly jabbing her in the face. Between that and the fact that she was staring at posters of hockey players and motor bikes on the wall, she'd try and keep her mind busy. When forced to kiss him, her stomach sickened at the thought of it and she pulled her lips away.

Jason grunted a few times. When it was over, he fixed his hat and climbed out of bed to go take a leak in the bathroom and throw his jeans back on. While he was in there, Dallas got herself dressed so that he wouldn't get a chance to see her naked and then she sat on the bed with her back and head leaning against the low headboard and wall behind.

She was silent as Jay spent a minute rummaging through some old metal army tins in one of the dresser drawers and came back to bed with a lighter, pipe and a small plastic bag with some weed in it. He cleaned out the screen at the end of the pipe with his fingernail, wiping off black residue on the bed and then he put a little bud in the end and lit it.

The two passed the pipe back and forth. For Jay, it was something he felt was cool. Dallas saw it as a way to escape what had just happened. They watched the beginnings of a movie in his room and then she left. Nights like this one were becoming pretty routine for them both.

Chapter XX-

Some years, October in Pine Creek was crisp and wintery. This year, it was stifling, humid and filled with long days where the sun took its time slipping below the shield of the pointed mountains. The creek was reduced to a lowly trickle and in the mornings, birds sang in eager anticipation of the winter months to come. The month was now drawing to a close and Halloween was just around the corner.

Clay stayed clear of his old school and did not share any information about the day he had been dragged with anyone at Stonebridge Academy. Classes resumed as if nothing had happened and his peers continued on as blind bats to the pain he had received.

The novel Mr. Kent had sent him was a great read. He had read the book in the first couple of days and was hoping Kent would send another soon. Set just after the Second World War, the story of travelling with intent to find meaning and belonging was not lost on Clay's consciousness. He too, was going through a personal war from which he desperately needed to escape.

Halloween in Pine Creek was a lot of fun for kids. Younger kids would be taken Trick-or-Treating by their parents in the early evening. Those in their early teens would head out just after 7pm. Most of them would head into the wealthier parts of town in the West where the best candy was handed out.

In Clay's neighborhood, people would either hand out the discount candy or they'd turn off all the lights in their houses pretending that no one was home so they wouldn't have to give away candy to the children when they rang the door buzzers. The high school kids would head out around 9pm just as the younger teenagers would be heading home. Only they had little intentions of Trick-or-Treating.

Some would get their share of candy by pillaging the younger kids who were desperately attempting to make their way home in the twilight, but most would be kept busy with acts of vandalism. Eggs and fireworks were the weapons of choice. Various teachers and administrators throughout the town would have their houses and cars egged. The remnants of egg shells, toilet paper rolls, smashed pumpkins, broken windows, and chipped or dented house siding and paintjobs, would be all that remained from the carnage when the sun rose the following morning.

Clay had been asked by Myles Carter and a few other kids from Stonebridge Academy to join them for the evening. The plan, as was customary each of the past few years, was for the graduating classes of the two rival schools to have a Roman candle war in the forest separating their territories. Typically, the fireworks used were long tubes which, when ignited, discharged a number of glowing balls of pyrotechnics. Soldiers, dressed in black, would retrieve tubes of various sizes and colors from their backpacks, light them, and shoot the hissing stars at their contemporaries.

There were rumors that one year a kid's hair had been caught on fire, though this urban legend was impossible to confirm with any level of certainty and it was far more common for direct hits to bounce off of their victims. Fearing fires were being started in the trees, eventually the police or fire department staff would show up and scare the teens off.

Clay had never taken part in any sort of battle before. In fact, he was so utterly non-competitive he would usually shy from anything of the sort. This year, he figured there would be safety in numbers and, besides, he didn't want to stay home knowing his place of residence was often the target of egg throwers.

He joined up with Myles and two of his pals from school at the fountain near Stonebridge Academy and then met the rest of the school's team at the edge of the forest. The large group of several dozen spoke of their attack plans and rendezvous points should they be separated. Clay listened intently but stood there in the blackness of the cloudy night trying to figure out what exactly he was supposed to be doing during the battle. The Stonebridge crew took off running.

Clay, still a bit dazed and confused, stayed close to Myles and his friends who stayed near the rear with a few other stragglers. Balls flew and screams of surprise were heard from up ahead deep in the trees where moonlit shadows of running teens mingled with those of the dry and needled branches of the conifers.

The moon slid behind another cloud darkening the forest further while small forces of three to four warriors spread out for

115

sneak attacks; some flanking the sides while others thought it was best to dive straight into the action. Glimpses of shadowy Pine Creek students whipped through the trees around them. Clay could make out sporadic streaks of light from the shooting fireworks surrounding him. Yells and curses were heard from both sides indicating people had made direct hits. Myles' buddies left the area with the last of the few Stonebridge kids in sight in pursuit of some noises they heard rustling in the brush.

"Come on," Myles said as he guided Clay through the darkness to one of the main trails acting like a branching artery in network of the forest. They jogged along the trail together for a couple minutes. Tree branches and spider webs kept catching them in the faces while they ran by.

They passed several kids along the route, some of which were calling "time out" as they walked from the brush and onto the trail while others sped along with the rush of adrenaline. Myles came up with a plan to ambush their public school enemies.

"Let's move just off the trail and hide behind these old logs." He pointed into the darkness and stepped off the path. Clay could just barely make out the silhouette of the weathered fir logs Myles had referred to. The two of them climbed over the dried bark of the decaying logs and crouched down just fifteen feet from the well-travelled route.

"We need to wait and be sure it's not our guys before we shoot." Myles handed Clay a lighter and a stick of fireworks.

Clay agreed and the two waited stealthily in the protection of the darkness. More than once, they were close to setting off their weapons before realizing they would be shooting at colleagues. One group of noisy Stonebridge troops stopped in front of their hiding spot to wait for a comrade to tie up his shoe. As they started off down the trail, a couple of stray enemies from Pine Creek Community School showed up to take their place. The two kids rested on the path right in plain view of the fallen logs and began strategizing about tracking those in front. Neither Myles nor Clay could make out who they were. Myles, using hushed hand gestures, signaled to Clay to light the fuses. But, it was the abrasive noise of Myles' lighter that momentarily caught the attention of the would-be prey.

"Oh shit!" one of them shrieked as the two snapped their heads back and forth looking for the source of the noise. Unable to locate anyone in the obscurity, they started off running like startled deer. Clay and Myles popped up from behind the logs and began firing their flares. It took the first couple of shots to get used to the small kick of the tube when the stars were released.

Holy smokes! This is crazy. This is crazy. This is crazy, Clay thought. He missed badly both times. The remaining shots whizzed by the Pine Creek prey narrowly missing. Myles, on the other hand, hopped over the log concealing him and started chasing the boys, firing shot after shot at his targets.

"Woo hoo! Die suckas!" Myles shrieked. Clay watched with admiration as Myles' accuracy was unrelenting. Two straight hits bounced off the back and triceps of the trailing kid, sizzling into the bushes. A third flew through the opening made between the boy's legs as he ran. A few steps further down the trail the boy was smacked in the face with a low overhanging branch. It made him stumble, wince and turn, spitting spruce needles out of his mouth. The boy's shoe started coming off as he dragged his foot and fell to the ground in the commotion. Myles stopped, stunned at the sight and in disbelief of his luck. He walked over to his downed opponent.

"Time out! Time Out! I'm down." the kid said. Clay ran towards them. He pulled up when he was close enough to recognize the face. The boy who sat in the dirt and spruce needles on the pathway struggled frantically to put his shoe back on without undoing the laces. Myles standing over him took aim and fired once more. A red ball discharged from the end of the tube. Clay heard the Pffffffp!

"What the hell? I was down." The red ball began to grow on the boy's side. It had not bounced off. Instead, it had stuck to his fleece pullover. The boy looked up at Myles with a worried look. Then, over at Clay. Clay, stunned, could make out Mark Mathies' face in the shadows.

"Jason, come back! They're here!" yelled Mark. Then, the screaming started. The hot ember melted through the fleece and began burning into Mark's ribs while he rolled around in the dirt slapping away at his side.

"Run!" Myles yelled. He turned, bumping into Clay as he took off down the trail. The bump woke Clay from his stupor and he too ran. The two teens sprinted all the way back to the fountain at the school. They arrived at the water feature in front of Stonebridge Academy tired and out of breath. Myles bent over, resting his hands on his knees, panting like a dog on a hot summer's day.

"What the hell are we going to do?" Myles asked.

"What can we do?" Clay replied. "We're dead. Things are going to get so much worse now. Soooo much worse. I don't know about you, but I'm going home." And with that, he left the fountain and hurriedly ran off.

Clay stayed up that night sitting in his bed and leaning against the headboard, thinking about the ordeal he had just been through and the resulting predicament it created for him. He knew from the sounds of the screams that Mark had been hurt and that Myles had been the one who had hit him at close range resulting in the burn. That was not what bothered him. After all, he didn't really care that much about Mark since he had been involved in the dragging incident and the flat tire scam. What worried him more than anything else was the fact that Mark had spotted him with Myles when it happened and that Jason would now have more fuel for the fire when it came to bullying him. Moving to the Academy did not solve all of Clay's problems and the bullying incidents were getting dangerously out of hand.

Chapter XXI-

The next morning, Clay arrived at Stonebridge and attended classes as usual; however, Myles did not show up to school. By noon, Clay decided he should swing by the office and ask if they'd heard anything. He could tell from the way the secretaries at the front desk looked at him that they had news but they told him they were unable to discuss someone else's personal matters with him directly.

Clay, being quick to think on his feet, replied "Myles asked me to pick up his homework if he couldn't get to school by lunch hour. I haven't seen him, so I assume he's not here."

Then, one of the ladies who seemed a bit confused based on the quizzical expression made by her cock-eyed eyebrows, all too eagerly shared the story. "Myles' father, Mr. Carter, called in to us at reception sometime around 9:00 this morning saying he had a spill on his bike and had to go to the hospital. It didn't sound like he would be attending school for at least the day."

"We're not sure how bad the accident was as Mr. Carter didn't say," said the other secretary. "But you should know this already, right? You spoke to him this morning didn't you? You must have if you knew he might not be back to school today."

Clay turned and left the desk without another word.

The receptionist called down the hallway after him, "Make sure you let us know if you hear from Myles. OK?"

Clay knew Myles had not fallen off of his bike on the way to school. *How bad could it be?* he thought. *I hope he's alright. I have to get ahold of him.*

Ever since he and Dallas had broken up, he hadn't had much use for his cell phone and he tended to leave it at home. He headed off to the library to use his email on one of the school computers. Clay sat down at a workstation and logged into his school email account. He knew Myles would have his phone with him and would quickly reply to any message if he was around.

Where r u? u OK?

He clicked Send. Moments later he had his response.

I'm alright. They jumped me just outside my place. Kicked me a few times and broke my ribs. Payback's a bitch.

Clay logged out as fast as he could, closed down the computer, and picked up his backpack. There was no doubt in his mind that Mark would be seeking revenge on him too just for being there on Halloween when it happened.

Leaving the library in sheer panic, he realised he had been holding his breath since he'd left the work station. He paused in the hallway just outside the library taking a second to breathe in and out thrice slowly to calm his nerves.

Like a stream of leaf cutter ants in the forest, students passed from both directions carrying papers, books, and backpacks. They were busily moving on from one class to the next, completely unaware of the tightness in his lungs. Again, he exhaled deeply then started off to class. He'd be safe there for the next couple of hours while surrounded by witnesses at school and he needed the time to figure out how to get home afterwards expecting them to be waiting for him at some point in his journey.

Clay tried not to think about the ordeal that took place on Halloween or about Myles during his biology and history classes. However, as the end of the school day was drawing closer, tension pulled at his neck muscles.

The math class was half empty when he arrived for his final period. His peers were turning the ringers off on their phones and using them to partially replace the voids left in their backpacks as they hauled out their texts and supplies. One by one, the rest of his class flowed into the room and took their seats. He sat there lost in his thoughts, which mixed feelings of fear, rage, and confusion.

Needing an escape plan, scenarios played out in his mind; each of them with disastrous endings involving him getting jumped and severely beaten up. His mind was flooded by flashback interruptions of the day he'd been dragged, Dallas telling him she'd rather be with Jason, and the events of Halloween. Clay's palms grew sweaty and he could feel himself feeling a bit lightheaded. He wiped the moisture from him palms on his thighs and knees under his desk trying to pull himself together as Mrs. Greenborough paced up between the aisles of desks toward him.

"Clay, are you alright?" Mrs. Greenborough asked. She was old and her face wore a tired smile that reflected years of patience with all too distracted youth. Her nose divided a set of wrinkles that heavily favoured the left side of her mouth where her smile rose more prominently. "Can you take out your stuff - we need to get started?"

Clay blinked hard a couple of times looking up and trying to focus on her wrinkled visage. Shaking his head slightly from side to side in an attempt to clear the slate, Clay leaned over the side of his desk and pulled his books from his bag. The leaning made him feel a little unbalanced and he decided he wasn't quite feeling a hundred percent.

Clay again looked up at his teacher and asked, "Can I go to the washroom?" figuring the act of getting a drink and splashing some water on his face might to help clear his thoughts enough to come up with a plan to get home alive.

"Go ahead, but please hurry back as I don't want you to miss the instructions for your next assignment," she said.

Clay pushed his chair out with the backs of his legs as he stood. Arranging his books on his desk to make it look like it mattered to him and that he'd be right back and get down to business working, he departed the classroom.

He walked past several other students on his way down the hall, most of them sitting on the floor against the lockers and working on their laptops. The bathroom was roughly halfway down the hallway that was lined with framed pictures connected to various activities the school had been involved with. He passed graduation photos and a framed jersey from a professional hockey player that had been autographed. Nobody from Stonebridge Academy had ever played professional hockey so it must have been purchased during some silent auction fundraiser by a wealthy parent and donated to the school.

The bathroom door swung open freely and banged against the brick wall behind. The room was cold and empty. A row of six pristine, ecofriendly, water-free urinals ran along one half of the back wall. The other half had stalls closing off four clean and new, cutting-edge, water-saving toilets. Signs were posted in front of the urinals and beside the large mirror which, being completely free from streaks and splatters, looked as though it had recently been cleaned.

Clay stepped up to the sinks and held his hands forming a cup shape under one of the taps. It turned on automatically and cool liquid filled his hands. He sipped a few cups and then splashed some of the water on his face gently patting his freckled cheeks. The drier was noisy as it blew with force over his wet hands; his face was dried with his shirt sleeve.

The door banged against the brick wall. Clay, startled, shuddered his shoulders as he twisted his head toward the sound. He had no idea how they got into the school or past the receptionists without being noticed or how they knew he was in this particular bathroom, but they had found him and he was not ready for it. They must have asked some of the kids scattered throughout the hallway. The students casually working would have had no reason not to tell them they had just seen him pass by. Jason grabbed Clay's left wrist with one arm and pushed him against the wall by the door with his other. He could feel the abrasiveness of the bricks behind him. Gripping his shirt collar and using a broad forearm, Jason pressed against Clay's neck, pinning his head against the stone.

"You shouldn't have done it. You should have stayed locked up in your house where you belong."

Mark followed Jason's lead, "You burned my guts you little faggot."

"I didn't do it. It wasn't me." Clay sputtered struggling to get the words out and still find enough air.

"Yeah, but you were there. I saw you. You ran like a little bitch, you chicken shit." Mark spat while he nudged in next to Jason so that he could get right into Clay's face. "We're going to play a game. It's called Flat Liner."

"Ha ha, always trying to hide. It's no use." Jason spun Clay around and Mark helped by pushing his face up hard against the wall.

He could feel the roughness of the cold stone scratching at his forehead.

"Trying to get away and live the big life at Stonebridge like it's the American dream. Well, if you wanna dream, I can put you to sleep, Tree Hugger." Jason pulled him slightly off the wall and wrapped an arm around his neck sinking an elbow just under the chin. The other arm swung around the other side to wrap around Clay's forehead.

Clay hunched his shoulders and clawed at the vines strangling his neck. There wasn't enough time to get a breath of air before Jason's arm tightened down. He could feel him re-adjust his grip a little and squeeze tighter like a constrictor with a small defenseless animal. Clay's shoulders dropped. Then his hands simultaneously followed.

He went under. There was no dream. No nightmare even. Just nothing.

"Hit 'em!" yelled Jason as he dropped the limp body to the ground and began waving his hands urging on violence like a fan at a British football match where the crowd had gone wildly out of control. "You owe him for what he did to you, man. Hit 'em!"

Mark took a combination lock out of his pocket and flipped it into his right hand, sliding his middle finger through the stainless steel loop and palming the large black rotating dial. Mark stepped closer and then straddled Clay's sleeping body on the floor. Clay's head rested unprotected wedged up against a horizontal pipe running along the wall. The impact from the lock and fist hitting his cheekbone snapped, and when combined with the thumping of his head bouncing off the floor, made the beginnings of a drum solo. Snap, thump, thump, thump. His cheek had been completely redisplayed with a large bump forming; opening up a gash in the shape of a crescent across the bone.

Mark and Jason left the washroom and arrogantly sauntered out of the school. There was no need to run. Nobody was coming and they weren't the least bit mournful of their actions.

Clay started to come to when he heard the bathroom door being kicked open hitting the wall behind again. The thump of the handle contacting the brick made him wince. He fluttered his eyes open worried the sound was another punch.

"What are you doing down there?" asked a boy standing in the doorway sharply dressed in full tie and school suit jacket. He surveyed the room for evidence of what had occurred but found none aside from the blood that was half clotted on Clay's cheek, dried thickly down to his neck and pooled on the tile floor below his ear. "Are you alright? Do you want me to get somebody? Did you fall?"

"Don't worry about it. I'm fine. I just fell." Clay reached for the sink and pulled himself stammering to his feet like a drunkard who had come off his bar stool. His balance was off for a moment but it cleared.

"Are you sure you want to stand up?

"Yeah. I'm fine, I said. What time is it?"

"The bell just went. Do you want me to get the nurse?"

"Quit asking so many questions," Clay snarled.

"Whatever. I was sent by Mrs. Greenborough to come check on you." The boy was a bit put off and with that, he walked past Clay and over to the urinal.

The broken young man stumbled over to the door bumping against the counter unexpectedly, causing him to realize he had not quite gained his balance back yet. He reached out and held the door handle for a second to steady himself before pulling it open and exiting.

He could tell from people wearing their coats and bags in the hallways that the school day had finished. It had been nearly a full period that he had been sprawled there on the bathroom floor unconscious. Clay wondered if that had been the first kid to use the washroom during the period, or if anybody else had seen him as well and just chose to go on with their business ignoring him on the floor.

The bus could quickly get him home where he could lie down but he'd have to face the embarrassment of everyone on the bus seeing the damage and blood on his face. He hadn't seen the damage personally; he hadn't taken the time in the washroom to look in the mirror. But based on the aching lumps he could feel on his head and the blood on his clothes, he knew it couldn't be good. There was no fear of walking home today. It would take him a while to get home especially as shaky as he was, but at least it would shelter him from questioning and ridicule. He chose not to go back to the math room to retrieve his books.

Chapter XXII-

Nursing injuries was never fun. Nursing broken souls was nearly impossible. When Clay's parents noticed the wounds on his face he was stunned. He hadn't expected them to notice; especially considering he had spent the entire evening in the solitary confinement of his room, but the next day when he didn't make his way to the kitchen to eat breakfast, Mrs. Morris actually came to find him still in bed in his room.

"Why haven't you eaten yet?" she asked softly. Her words were clear enough that Clay could tell she hadn't taken any medication today.

"I'm not feeling well," he said trying to turn away without her noticing why.

She stared at the lump on his cheek like it offended her.

"What happened to you?" There seemed to be genuine concern in her voice.

"I fell off my bike on my way home from school." He knew she wouldn't have heard the same lie that Myles had used convincingly on his own parents.

"I didn't know you still rode that old bike. Are you OK?" She came closer, stepping over the pile of clothes which included his bloody shirt, and examined the mark as she sat down on the corner of the bed.

He turned his cheek toward her, happy inside to finally be receiving attention for once. She held his face gently in her hand and looked closely at the cut. "What did you hit?"

"I think it was the handle bars."

"I'll get you some ice and your breakfast. You can stay home today and I'll call the school." She stood up from the edge of the bed and left the room.

Clay couldn't believe it. His mother was caring for him. Warmth grew inside him while he ran his index finger along the side of his face touching the spot where his mother had held him.

Mrs. Morris came back up the stairs a few minutes later carrying an old tray. A bowl filled with cereal and milk was on one side. Next to it, sat a spoon underneath a bag of frozen mixed vegetables. On the other edge of the tray sat a thick brown envelope. He recognized the tape job.

"We didn't have any ice so I think this will have to do for you." She set the tray on his dresser and passed him the bag of vegetables. "After you numb it with the vegetables, you may want to clean it up a bit better than that."

Clay hadn't yet washed off the dried blood but he had gooped on some antibiotic ointment that he had found in the medicine cabinet last night before going to bed. It had smeared across his cheek and onto his earlobe.

"Thanks. I think I'll eat first though." He was torn between wanting her to stay by his side and wanting her to leave so that he could open the envelope he knew was from Mr. Kent.

His mother made the choice for him. "I'll leave you to rest and I'll go phone the school." Mrs. Morris quietly shut the door to his room behind her.

Clay pulled the covers back enough that he could climb over to the edge of his bed where he could reach the tray, grabbing the book before sitting back down. Mr. Kent's penmanship was on the front in thick black ink. He peeled enough of the tape off piece by piece until he could wiggle a couple of fingers in the top of the envelope to pry it open. This time two books slid out with some thick magazine-like brochures. There was no note from Kent this time. The books, *Into the Wild* by Jon Krakauer and *Never Cry Wolf* by Farley Mowat intrigued him and he knew they'd be right up his alley.

The glossy brochures immediately stole away his attention. Clay read the covers. One was from a university in the city fairly close to home. He tossed it aside- not because the university wasn't well known to offer solid programs, but because it wasn't far enough away from this place. The second one, Undergraduate Admissions: University of Oxford, he began to read thoroughly.

The next day was Friday. Clay spent it, and the entire weekend that followed, at home in bed reading. One of the novels inspired him with its themes of individual uprising and the escape from a society of oppressive individuals, while the other dealt with the idea of isolation; something Clay was all too familiar with. It seemed every time he was feeling at his absolute lowest, Mr. Kent would send him just the right words of inspiration through his selection of book titles.

His mom had checked on him intermittently and had been sufficiently concerned to bring him breakfast, lunch and dinner each day. This had really helped to speed up his recovery. He had not seen his father but expected that his dad had worked straight through the weekend.

He returned to school on Monday with a face resembling a rainbow of colors but with a fairly positive attitude. His mom's interest and Mr. Kent's book selections had brought him back to life.

Chapter XXIII-

Hockey training and games filled Jason's spare time and he continued to play well by mixing scoring with enough penalty minutes to let people know he could do it all. Dallas was by his side each day putting up with his sexist comments to his friends and other forms of cruelness that she had readily and sadly become accustomed to.

His marks were firmly held in the passing range just to maintain any possible scholarship opportunities. Of course, Leon and Billy were sure to help with cheating whenever necessary. Just as Pine Creek Community High School was dropping into the regularity of the fall term, Jason stopped showing up for school for a solid week. Nobody heard anything from him and he was not answering calls or returning text messages from any of his friends or from Dallas.

In the third week of November, Jason showed up to school one morning with crutches. He had inadvertently collided with an opponent crossing center ice during a tournament. Aside from those involved in the game, only Dallas had been there to see it. The knee on knee impact smashed his patella and caused his anterior cruciate ligament, one of the four main ligaments in the human knee, to tear completely. He had spent the week in the hospital undergoing emergency surgery to repair the damage. He had also spent the week coming to terms with the fact that his dreams of playing hockey were gone forever and the surgery was done merely to preserve his ability to walk properly for the rest of his life. A dejected, Dallas Hilton was as devastated with the injury news as he was.

News of the injury travelled through the hockey league with the speed of the internet and it wasn't long before Jason received contact from the University of Michigan that his scholarship offers had been revoked due to the uncertainty of his health. The other schools that were at the table soon followed suit.

Chapter XXIV-

It took Clay a couple of days into December to realize that his father hadn't been around much. He wondered if the office had been keeping him late each night. Mr. Morris left for work early every morning, so normally Clay would never see him until quite late in the evening, if he even saw him at all. At busy times of the year, his father would take on a lot of additional shifts to earn the minimal extra pay that went along with overtime hours to help make ends meet at home.

Perhaps, Clay wondered, *his absence over the past few days had been due to this overworking.* Once an entire week had rolled by and Clay had seen no sign of his dad, he began to wonder what was up and if he had been asked to travel somewhere for work. Mr. Morris never had to travel for work, but by now Clay was grasping at straws to figure out the reason for his absence.

Mrs. Morris, on the other hand, continued with her aberrant conduct in that she not only cooked and tidied up around the house, but she was outspoken in her conversations with her son. Strangely, she was acting as if the clock had been reversed to a time before his brother had died. It had been one of the greatest months of Clay Morris's life. She had been asking about school, questioning him on whether he had completed all of his assigned homework, asking what he thought of the nightly meal, and generally conversing with him about his day to day whereabouts.

Clay began to notice her lack of focus on discussing certain family members. Not once had she noted Mr. Morris in her choice of conversational topics.

"Dad sure has been working a lot lately," Clay said one evening after dinner while flipping through channels. His mother sat on the chesterfield nearby, reading a gardening magazine while he probed her for answers regarding his father's absenteeism.

"Clay? I've got to tell you something." She closed her magazine and shifted her position so that she was turned toward him.

"What?" He had no idea what was coming.

"Your father and I have had some difficulties lately." Mrs. Morris was now fiddling with the edges of her magazine and her gaze dropped to the floor for a moment before returning to meet with her son's.

Clay expected her to inform him of their family's financial woes; however, these issues weren't exactly news to him. "Like what?" Clay, a bit afraid to ask, but more curious than ever about what was going on, muted the television and put the remote control in his lap.

"Your father has left me." Clay felt the words as if a shotgun had fired from close range and hit him square in the chest. Breathing became laborious and his mind swirled with dizziness as he attempted to comprehend the news. "He hasn't left you though, Clay." There was silence.

He was sure he hadn't heard her correctly. His parents had been through good times and bad. Sure they had some serious fights now and then, but certainly not in the past few years; it was difficult to fight when you were barely speaking to one another. He must have misinterpreted her.

"Clay?... Did you hear what I just said?" Again she shifted uneasily in her seat. "Your father has left me. He is staying at a friend's from work until we can figure things out."

"You mean... like, when he's going to come home?" Clay paused to breathe deeply. "He is coming home, right?"

"He hasn't left you, Clay. He wanted me to tell you that." Mrs. Morris moved to her opposite hip, unable to find a comfortable position on the couch.

Given the fact that his father was no longer staying in the home where his son lived, it sure as hell felt like he was leaving him. Clay was selfish in his thoughts. He didn't care if his father came back for his mother, but he shouldn't have left him. *He couldn't have left me without saying goodbye.* Clay's throat squeezed around his Adam's apple.

"He didn't even say goodbye." Clay began to tear up but wiped away the opportunity with his shirt sleeve. He could feel knots forming in his stomach. They were quickly forgotten as he was forced to switch his concentration to keeping his throat open, which now sealed tighter than when Jason had squeezed it. This hurt more.

Mrs. Morris began to cry and she clenched the magazine in her fist making it unreadable. Her softness was more evident now as she used her thumb to pull a long strand of hair off of her face after it had been held there by tears slipping from the corner of her eye.

Understanding was written all over his face, but inside Clay was deeply hurt. *How could she have let his father leave? What could she possible have done to make him go?* His emotions made it difficult to think straight. *What could she possibly have done to make him stay?* He felt sorry for her now. She had been so cold for so long that her tears were not something he was used to seeing. Clay sniffled and he swallowed hard trying to regain enough control over his throat to speak. *Life is not fair.*

"I'm sorry mom." As much as it hurt him to know that this was the reason for her out of character, caring behavior, he was willing to accept it; the alternative of her going cold and closing him out again was no better. He hoped his words would make her stay with him- stay the way she had been for the past few weeks. Even if it was a forced hand serving as a reaction to his father's leaving.

She moved out of her chair and over to where her son was sitting. He stood, not sure what else to do. When she hugged him he could hold back the tears no further and they started to flood his eyes so much that it was difficult to see. He wrapped his arms around his mother and closed his eyes tightly; water dripping from his gritted eyes onto his shirt. *A Change is Gonna Come*, he thought. This was one he had neither expected nor hoped for and it was going to take a while to accept.

"Your father will be back in a few days to collect some stuff and sort out some money with me. Not sure if you want to be here for that. He wanted me to tell you before he came back. Otherwise, if you're up for it, I'm sure it would be OK if you called him."

He should be the one calling me, Clay reeled back pulling himself free from his mom's embrace and angered at the thought that had just crossed his mind. He could feel himself getting fired up so he decided it was best if he cut the moment short. "I'm going to go up to my room."

"Okay."

The end of term came fairly quickly considering the snowy weather in Pine Creek had forced Clay to hold up in his house for most of what was left of December and the entire winter break, which was all completely socially uneventful; even by Clay's meager standards. He had spent a few hours here and there over Christmas with his father who was still staying in a spare room at his friend's house. The fact that he was now paying his friend monthly rent, suggested to Clay that there was little intent for his father to get a place of his own, so Clay spent the majority of his time at home with his mother.

Chapter XXV-

With the budding concern that Jason would likely never play hockey in the big leagues and thus, never leave Pine Creek, Dallas Hilton had begun to try and make other arrangements. Her risky move in leaving Clay for Jason, who seemed like a sure thing at the time and someone of nobler prowess in town, was proving to be a poor decision. Dallas strongly hoped that Clay would take her back. If she could tag on to him and make him feel that he loved her, he might just ask her to come with him should he leave. And even more so in the New Year, Clay looked to be a man on a mission to take the fast track out of town.

Dallas approached the screen door at Jason's house a little later than usual. He had texted her a message; most of it, other than a request for her to come by around 11:00pm, had made little sense. The letters were scrambled and his choice of words seemed strange.

He must have started smoking up earlier than normal, she thought to herself. Hopefully it would mellow him out enough that she could dump him quickly and get the hell out of the house before he raged out of control. She knew his temper and it wasn't pretty. It was like trying not to wake a sleeping dragon.

Shaking her head in disbelief of the daunting task ahead of her, she searched for the hole in the screen through which she could fish her hand to unlock the inner door. As she found the lock and pulled her hand back through the wire mesh, she rubbed against the screen scratching the softness of the underside of her wrist. A small bead of blood developed where the thin threads of metal had clawed her and it slowly dripped onto the soiled Welcome mat on which she stood in the darkness.

Could be worse, she thought as the drop began to freeze onto the bristles of the mat.

She unlocked the door and stepped through onto the landing before closing it behind her as quietly as possible. She did not want to wake his parents as that would just piss him off more. Her feet were silent as she carefully selected stairs she thought were less squeaky on the way down to his room.

Jason stood there at the bottom holding the door open. When she got down the stairs, she leaned in to give him a kiss. Jay waited until she was close enough and then blew smoke in her face. He coughed a few times before laughing and moving into his sanctuary.

What a dick, Dallas glared at him as he turned his back toward her. The smell of marijuana filled the air and she waved it away from her face when she walked in.

He picked up a can of air freshener and sprayed it in an arc across the room with a large circular sweep of his outstretched arm. There was no way that it was going to cover up the overwhelming smell in there. He had obviously started really early today. There were also a couple of empty cans of energy drinks on the rug by his bed. A fine mix of stimulants and depressants just to keep it interesting while he played video games; the first person image of a gunman's arms holding a sawed off shotgun with a view of a busy city street in front of him flickered on the screen.

Jay sat down on the edge of his bed. "You want some?" He held out a pipe and a lighter, the pipe small and shaped like a bullet, the lighter a cheap one but something he had on him at all times. "I got a new pipe and figured I should try it out."

"No thanks. Not tonight," her words were under spoken as they held in the smoky air.

"Suit yourself. It's good shit," he reassured himself. "I bought it straight from Vic. He gave me a deal 'cause I got so much this time." Vic was the local dealer; an older looking guy, long haired, tattooed, and worn, who had spent his years playing music in one of the fruitful bars that catered nightly to bikers and loggers. Jay was proud of the fact that he had demonstrated to Vic that he'd been working up a tolerance for the stuff. "So are we gonna do it or what?" He put the pipe and lighter down on the floor.

Isn't he a romantic? Dallas thought sarcastically. Dallas hadn't really thought through how the whole encounter was supposed to go and wasn't sure where to take it from here. She figured she could stall until she could find the right time to tell him. Spontaneous and un-wanted sex with Jay was nothing new for her and it had never had any physical appeal.

"Take off your pants and lay back on the bed so we can get started," she said.

He obliged and removed his shirt as well, laying there in just his ball cap and dirty socks. She thought of the easiest and fastest way to get the job done. Kneeling down beside the mattress she grabbed him with her hand. It took him longer than usual to stiffen.

Damn weed, she thought as she used her hand to bring him to climax a short while later. *I hate myself for doing this.*

Dallas got up and walked to the bathroom to wash her hands. Jay used his shirt to clean up the mess and then threw on his pants and grabbed another canned energy drink off the end table beside the bed before she was back.

Now or never, she thought. "I'm leaving you." She recoiled inside as the words left her lips. *Did he hear me?* She stood wondering if she needed to repeat herself. On the outside she stood firm and unbothered by the attention she was now receiving. She lifted her chin and looked at him in the eye for a split second in a defiant way that announced she did not fear him.

Jason turned as if to put the can back on the night stand, but turned back violently and cracked her across the face with it. The back of his hand made contact as the liquid splashed and flew out of the can and across the room.

She staggered and then regained her footing and stood up straighter than before. "Is that it?" as if to challenge him.

"Do you want it to be?" he accepted the challenge and raised his hand once again to threaten her. "I don't need you. I just used you to get off. Now get out of here you dumb slut."

The words hurt her more that his cheap shot had. They stabbed at her heart and caused the throbbing pain to come from the inside out so that they welled up as tears in her hazel eyes. Dallas headed for his bedroom door and he began to follow like a prison guard escorting an inmate.

"Hurry the hell up. Get out of here." He chased her heels up the stairs giving her little time to grab her coat, open both sets of doors and step out onto the front step. Jason slammed the heavy door behind her so hard that the screen door rattled back open afterwards.

Looking down at the Welcome mat, Dallas leaned over and spat a wash of blood filled saliva. It was the second time she has spilled blood on the mat tonight. Dallas realized she may have jinxed herself when she had dripped blood on the mat on the way in- *It did get worse.* She used the inside edge of her shoe to smear the blood across the letters on the mat before grinding it in with her toes. "You're Welcome. Asshole!" She stepped down from the stairs and trudged home in the gloomy shadows.

Dallas was not about to waste any time trying to get back together with Clay. A block away from Jay's house, she pulled her smart phone out of her coat pocket and swiped her finger across the screen to reveal a picture of her holding a small fuzz ball of a cat, and the time, which read 11:28pm. *Well that didn't take long. Hopefully this goes a bit better.* Her fingers were cold in the wintry air. Tapping on the screen, she sent the message:

Hey Clay! U Awake?? ;P

She kept walking in the direction of the trailer park where she lived assuming he would be asleep already and not respond.

What do u want?

He replied, his inexperienced fingers barely nimble enough to text back.

Can I come over? (. Y .)

No

This was going to take more work than she had anticipated. He didn't even bite on the image she made with symbols strategically placed in her text. Dallas walked home and went to bed thinking about how she could get Clay to take her back.

Lying there awake, still playing through the incident with Jay in her mind and proud of the fact that she took it on the chin- quite literally- she grabbed her phone off of the dresser and reread the sequence of emails to Clay. Prepared to make another bold decision and ready to make a risky move in the digital era where messages were passed to and fro between recipients at the speed of light, she felt she had nothing to lose and everything to gain.

Provocative photos were no longer used for blackmail and they were too readily accessible to anyone at any time with WiFi, but they were still a valued currency. She took off her shirt and, looking down at her breasts, she unfastened her red-laced bra from the back and slipped her arms through before flicking it onto the floor. Then she held out her phone and snapped a shot.

Dallas glanced at the screen for a moment, knowing that if she stared too long she'd change her mind, then gave a naughty smile, doubled checked that Clay's address was the only recipient listed, and clicked: SEND.

Stopping the transfer of the digital file now was impossible. Her second thoughts had come too late and she was worried she'd eventually regret this move. The image made its way through cyberspace to Clay in a fraction of a second.

Are you sure? Tomorrow then?

Clay did not receive the message until the following morning when he checked his phone. Stunned to say the least, Clay admired the photo for a few minutes dreaming of the girl in the image and thinking back to the past year when he was as much hers as she was his. Forced to struggle with the contradicting thoughts, he was torn with whether or not he should keep the image. He hated her for what she did to him and he wasn't going to buy into any story this girl told him. Though the sexting of the image was strange, Dallas was demonstrating a certain amount of trust in Clay by sending it to him. Clay knew she had a reputation at school, but he also knew through his time with her last summer, that it was unwarranted. She was not the bad girl everyone made her out to be. She, like he and

Jason, just wanted some respect and there was no way to get any in this town. Her backwards means of getting respect by sending the image of herself was not a cry for help, but a strategic move to place her in a position to increase her odds of moving on from Pine Creek under someone else's accord.

Clay was having none of it. He was too badly hurt when she left him and the picture would only prolong the agony of being heartbroken. Whatever lack of faith he had, he did not lack in morals. The young man closed the topless picture file of his ex-girlfriend and texted her back:

Leave me alone

Dallas read the message and knew that she needed to speak to him in person. When she called his house, Clay's mother informed her that Clay had gone off to the public library to review for midterms.

She would find him there sitting on an uncomfortable looking orange plastic chair at a round table. Clay was taking a break from studying math. When he noticed Dallas walking over to his study area, he put down one of the novels Mr. Kent had sent him and pretended to be in the middle of some complex calculations. She pulled up a chair and sat down beside him.

"What do you want?" Clay asked, not even bothering to look up.

"Did you get my message?"

"I deleted it." Clay knew it was a lie but he wanted to make a point.

"Can we go somewhere to talk?" Dallas was desperate now and Clay could hear it as her soft voice trembled behind the curtains of her bangs swathed across the front of her face.

"I'm not interested in talking to you right now."

"Please. I miss you, Clay." He figured this lie on her part was enough to cancel the lie of his own.

"I'm not with Jay anymore. Can we go talk?"

"I said No!" Clay yelled uncharacteristically, drawing the attention of other people in the library. Dallas could feel their eyes on her. Her self-conscious nature made the glares from their eyes seem more than just a little uncomfortable and she took the hint.

That was it for Dallas. She got up and left the table and Clay made no attempt to stop her. She fought back the tears as she walked out of the library feeling everyone's eyes focused on her. As she stood on the chipped concrete steps of the building she noticed Jay driving by in Mark's truck. They honked and Mark gave her the finger out the window from his driver's seat.

Depressed and feeling resented, she stood there with a vacant look in her eyes. *I wish I was instantly alone in my room where I could cut myself.* The thought of being able to release her stress in the only way she knew how offered no consolation to her in front of the library. Jay had definitely noticed her. Now she not only felt bad that she had left Clay the first time, but she was upset for leaving

Jay. Perhaps she could have stuck it out with him? *Nope. Definitely not.*

The photo scared her too. *What if he hadn't deleted it?* What was sent could never be unsent. *He could do anything he wanted with that shot.* She came to the painful realization that her judgment about photos being used as blackmail was now totally premature. The thought hung heavy on as she went home in the January frost.

What Dallas had not known was that Jason and Mark had been parked outside the library for a while. When she dumped Jason and left his basement suite the night before, he had been flooded with emotions as he drifted off to sleep. In the morning, Jason was torn between wanting her back and being incredibly angry she had left him. His injured knee was also still bothering him so he had decided to call up Mark to hang out and get his mind off of things. The two of them had decided to head to the lakeshore to do some ice fishing and drink a few beers he had stolen from his parents.

Mark had picked him up and, in passing the library on their way to the lake, they had spotted Dallas going inside. Jason had asked Mark to pull his truck over to the side of the road so they could spy on her through the library's large exterior wall of windows. From their vantage point in the truck, they could see the impromptu meeting taking place between Dallas and Clay. This prompted some jealous anger and it was enough to set Jason's temper off again and they sped away in the truck just as she was leaving the library in tears.

Chapter XXVI-

Dallas and her friend, Jenn, sat facing each other at one of the red metal tables at the far side of the cafeteria just behind a couple of large support beams. This table was their usual spot for lunch; a few feet from the outside wall and far enough away from others. With Jenn's back to the wall and Dallas's toward the support posts, they could stare at other students as they ate and chat in peace about whatever they wanted.

Their orange food trays were littered with scraps of deep fried chicken strips and the over-crisp ends of French fries and they were pushed off to the side of the table so that the girls could share gossip about other girls and boys. Jenn, the only female Dallas ever really enjoyed hanging out with at school, came from a modest family that never shorted her on new outfits to wear during the school year. She didn't drive either and lived quite a ways from Dallas which made it nearly impossible for the two of them to ever hang out together outside of school time.

A brunette with shoulder length ringlets of finely primped, silky hair, Jenn stood out in school with her stunning looks. Incessantly worried about her own appearance, she was pleased to keep Dallas around, knowing that Dallas's individualized sense of style and her milder effort with regards to personal upkeep only made her own high society fashion sense stand out with more vigor when people would see and compare the two of them together.

Three students passed by their table and dumped the scraps of food that were left on their trays in a nearby garbage can before heading out an exit door just behind where Dallas and Jenn sat. Both girls tracked the group with their gazes and assessed each individual's choice in clothes as they passed.

Jenn made it a regular habit to trash talk other students for what they had chosen to wear each day. That was something Dallas really detested about Jenn but there was no way she would mention it to her for fear of offending her and causing her to lose the one girl she even sort of liked.

Dallas didn't spend much time with Jenn outside of school, but she was someone who was tolerable and worth killing time with during their drab classes. As Dallas pretended to snicker after Jenn's comments, she failed to notice Mark and Billy slipping back in to the school through the side exit door just as the three other students had left.

The boys sat down at a table on the opposite side of the support beams. Not realizing the closeness of their company, the girls sat chatting for some time before Jenn brought up the topic of Clay and Jason. Dallas kept most of it to herself; however, she did open up about spending the summer with Clay. She spoke not only of the time they had spent hanging out but also about having sex with him for the first time. Jenn prodded Dallas for further juicy details but Dallas was well restrained on the subject.

Mark and Billy's ears had perked up and the two were listening intently, knowing they were privy to some private

151

conversation that would be of interest to at least one of their friends. They held in their giggles and snickers for a bit longer deciding they should try and sneak out undetected if given a chance. Then, Dallas mentioned dumping Jay with hopes of getting back together with Clay. Mark and Billy took that last piece of information as their cue to get up and move on before being noticed.

The boys stood up quietly and left unseen through the exit door they had just come in. It was starting to snow lightly outside. The fresh snow left a light film over the crusted icy layer of older snow beneath. They had to share the news with Jason before lunch was over. Running through the school yard, down Heartbreak Hill, and across the track, they found Jason hanging out with Leon, Nathan and William huddled up in the lightly blowing snow by the uprights of the football field. They had gone there so that William could smoke a cigarette without being seen by school personnel.

The school didn't even have a football team any more. It had dissolved years ago when the initial batch of equipment from the 1980's had worn out and the school had refused to pay for new gear because of what they deemed to be an impractical cost for a non-essential program.

The boys jogged over to where their friends stood and when Mark began to explain what they had just overheard, Billy blasted out the punch line of the discussion.

"What did you say?" Jason asked, his attention snapping his neck around so he was looking right at Billy who stood there panting from the run and the cold air.

"D-D-Dallas… Clay… J-J-Jenn…" Billy stuttered. He had skipped his meds again today.

Mark, who was clearing some snow from around his ankles stepped in, "We overheard Dallas and Jenn in the cafeteria talking about you." Mark was trying to find a way to break the news to Jason like a politician. "She broke up with you because she wants that kid, Clay, back. They were together all summer, I guess."

"Who cares," Jason said trying to save face in front of the other boys watching him closely for a response. Besides, this news wasn't really anything he didn't already know. "But I'm still gonna kill that kid if I see him again." *No bitch dumps me for that guy.* Jason could feel the anger raging through him like a dozen energy drinks. He gritted his teeth making the scar across his face more prominent. *I'm going to break that kid in half the next time I see him. I'll cave in his head. Then she can have him.*

The bell rang in the distance causing their attention to be diverted. William, seemingly oblivious to Jason's anger, used the buzzer as a cue to change the subject to how much he hated his next class. Jason was fine with letting the conversation drop. He had some thinking to do during his classes that afternoon. He bent down and rubbed at the soreness on the side of his knee; the cold air causing it to ache more than normal. *I've gotta figure this out*, Jason thought, blocking out the rambling conversation of his peers. Math and English were sleepers anyhow and he had already planned on skipping Latin. Jason felt that he might still have one last shot at escaping the dreadful town. It would mean he would have to pull off some substantial marks in his classes to get into college.

I have to get into college, he was now dwelling on the thought. Any college, the thought held fast to a place deep in his mind. In any other town but Pine Creek. I need to get better marks so I can get out of this place. And I'll need a job to pay for school, but I'll deal with that later. First, I'll have to cheat my way in to college.

Given the weight of his final exams taking place in a few months, it was possible for him to get accepted into some colleges if he performed well enough on the tests to bring his marks up a bit further- and that would take some serious planning in terms of how best to cheat his way through the system. He was confidently up for the task as he and his clan made their way back through the snow into the school.

Chapter XXVII-

"We're out of milk, Clay," Mrs. Morris said as her son came downstairs for breakfast one warm Saturday morning in early spring. "I'll make you some pancakes if you run out and pick up a carton from the 7-11."

Clay loved his new mom. She had continued to be someone who actually cared about him after his father had left. It had been long enough now that Clay was beginning to doubt if it was actually a charade. *Perhaps, she really was happier without his dad around?* he wondered.

Maybe it was easier for her to forget about his brother without his dad at home. Neil always did look more like dad. Clay missed his brother and father dearly, but blocked out any further memories before they could upset him. "Sure mom. I can go to the store. No problem," he said.

"Do you need some money?"

"No, I have some," he replied.

"Here, take this and pick up some toilet paper too while you're there. We're out. Oh, and some toothpaste too." She handed him a scrunched up old twenty dollar bill.

"Alright," Clay said as he laced up his shoes. *Just what I need- carrying around a bunch of toilet paper through the neighborhood like some idiot. At least she didn't ask me to get some tampons.* He swung open the screen door, hopped down the stairs at the front of the house and started off down the sidewalk. As he kicked a small rock along the cracked cement in front of himself, he began to wonder if any of the streets he'd walk down in his life could ever take him anywhere but Pine Creek.

The convenience store was only four or five blocks away and it was open all day long. At this time of the morning it was likely he'd be the only one in there and he could make it back home in less than fifteen minutes.

The glass door chimed as he opened it. It played a tune and, though it was all of five notes, it was just enough to let you know that you were welcome in. He was the only one there; except for the cashier. The grey haired figure counting quarters behind the tall orange and green striped counter was an elderly man who had likely taken on the job to supplement his measly retirement income. The night shift had made him tired and he had barely enough voice to say,

"Good morning," as Clay walked past the counter.

"Good morning," Clay replied. He turned down the aisle with the household items and grabbed the one and only brand of toothpaste available. It came in a small, travel-sized box which he felt was very over priced for the amount in it. Then he shuffled a bit further down to grab a bundle of toilet paper wrapped in plastic packaging. This enormous bag easily made up for the toothpaste shortfall. Again, it was the only size they carried in the store and it most certainly cost a fortune. Making his way to the back of the store, he opened the large sliding doors of the cooler and grabbed a carton of milk. The glass door slammed shut, sending a puff of steam out from the cold storage shelves within.

Clay proceeded to the counter and paid for the items with the cash from his mother before stuffing the change back into his wallet, bidding the man farewell and heading out the door. The slender teen tucked the plastic package under one arm and held on to the milk and toothpaste in the other. It was awkward but he didn't have far to walk. He made it about a block before they spotted him.

They arrived at the store shortly after he had, looking to grab some junk food and Leon spotted him through the main glass door right as he was about to open it. The group decided it would be best not to get into anything in the store as they had had issues with the old man catching a few of them shoplifting when they were younger. Instead, they watched Clay through the windows while he picked up the items and then they hid around the corner of the building when he exited. A perfect ambush.

The boys let him walk a little way from the store before they ran up on him. The attack occurred before Clay could even notice and the group circled him like a pack of hunting dogs. The horde was hungry and Jason, the alpha dog who had been waiting for weeks for a moment like this, was the first to strike.

He hit Clay with a bare, iron heavy fist. The punch landed a bit higher than Jason had intended because of the fact that Clay instinctively tried to block it by turning his head and raising his shoulder. This reflex had caused Jason's hand to glance off of the package of toilet paper before finding the thin edge of bone lining

157

the upper crest of his prey's left eye socket. It was slightly off the mark but damaging. The skin split along the eyebrow wide enough that one could see the bone below for just a moment before it welled up with blood.

Leon kicked out the back of Clay's knee, dropping him to the ground and sending his purchases crashing down beside him. They weren't even courteous enough to take turns punching him and they rained down like a thunder cloud. Both eyes were bleeding so much now that they were interfering with his vision and he couldn't see who was doing what. He tried to cover up using his forearms but a couple of kicks moved them aside before splitting open his cheek and knocking free a molar on that side.

At one point, things went dark before Jason had the toothpaste idea. Jason had noticed the box sitting on the sidewalk and, while the others continued to bang away at Clay's face and head, he had removed the small tube inside and twisted its cap off. Then, he ordered the others to stand aside while he shoved the end of the tube up Clay's nostril as far as he could push it. With a slap of both hands on either side of the tube, Jason emptied its contents into Clay's sinuses.

"Let's beat the crap out of him." William thought he was funny as he kicked him a few more times in the ribs and said, "At least you have toilet paper." Once he noticed the rest of the group was already leaving, he stopped and chased off after them down the street.

Clay never felt any of it. He was already out. Milk poured from the carton lying next to his head mixing with the blood seeping from his face. The pooling mixture at the edge of the sidewalk was a pinkish blush color for a few seconds before taking on a darker red hue.

The old man from the store found him half on the sidewalk and half on the road. His shift had ended a little while after Clay had left the store and once he had finished cleaning up from the night and transferring over the keys to a co-worker, he had gotten in his car and was heading home.

Apparently he had used the better part of the package of toilet paper trying to stop the bleeding before the ambulance arrived. "Must have been clipped by a car," he said, naive to what had happened. The paramedics were fooled briefly too until they noticed the toothpaste.

Chapter XXVIII-

Clay's mother received a phone call from the hospital to come down to retrieve her son. Doctors in the emergency room had done a good job of putting him back together and cleaning him up. Even so, she had difficulty recognizing him when she first entered the room. He was heavily bandaged and they had shaved a small patch of hair back past his ear on the left half of his head so they could put in a few staples. His cheekbone was badly bruised and several sets of sutures had been used to close various gashes that crisscrossed his cheeks, brow line and forehead. Clay's nose had been straightened but it laid buried deep in the swelling of his lips and eyes which had taken on blue and black tones like he had been starved of oxygen. There were no witnesses she was told. And they still weren't entirely sure it wasn't a hit and run with a vehicle. Only Clay would be able to fill them in on the truth.

And he wasn't going to. After being released from the hospital, Clay's mom nursed him for several days at home. It was about a week before he was able to return to school. Clay refused to speak about the incident and his mother, seeing how much it hurt him, did not press for answers as the days flew by and spring edged its way closer to summer and the end of another school year.

Chapter XXIX-

The dreaded final exam weeks at the end of the year for both Pine Creek Community High School and Stonebridge Academy seemed quickly approaching. There was still time, but Jason needed at least some of those tests to ensure he'd graduate with high enough marks to get accepted into a college. They would be worth half of the grades for their respective courses and a strong result on those tests would ensure he did well in the classes that could make or break his graduation.

Bringing in and effectively using cheat sheets with enough information required to ace any possible question would be too difficult for Jason to pull off repeatedly for each individual test; especially when the material would cover everything they had received instruction on from September to June. He and his friends were going to have to steal him the exams. The process by which they came across and took other exams during the year had proved very successful; however, these were final exams and stealing them would be more difficult as they were always kept protected in filing cabinets in teachers' locked offices, as per school protocol for assessment tools of this nature. Jason was going to have to break into each faculty member's office separately and, to do this, he would require help from his friends. In return, they would all be happy and eager to receive the answers to the exam questions themselves.

Ever since the school budget had been cut, there had been little funds left over for janitorial duties. This is part of the reason the school had become so run down in such a short time frame. Only two custodial staff were employed at Pine Creek Community High School and they worked shift work. One would work the day shifts while school was in session and the second would work the evening shift.

They were going to have to observe the janitors over the next few days to sort out when and where they'd be at any given time during the night. This information would be easy enough to gather and it would hold the key to accessing the building after hours without setting off any alarms and getting into the offices of the teachers undetected.

Mark and Billy stayed late each and every afternoon for the next week; at first in the library or gymnasium until all of the faculty and students had left and the school was being locked up, and then later they'd move undetected into the hallways or classrooms paying close attention to when the janitors came on shift and when they departed. There was no risk of being heard as the night cleaner wore a head set the entire shift and listened to music while she worked. They documented the changing of the guard which occurred at precisely 4:00pm; sometimes the one on shift prior to that would actually pack it in as early as 3:50pm and the second shift that was supposed to be completed at midnight would often conclude shortly after 11:00pm if the staff on duty felt so inclined to work a bit harder during her shift so as to complete all of her duties ahead of her standard quitting time. Though not one to bank on, leaving early was a fairly regular occurrence and nobody other than Mark and Billy was ever the wiser.

The janitor would only ever set the school's alarm as she left the building for good at the end of the night. The rest of the evening the alarm was not in use. After receiving a brief run through of any important information being passed on from her counterpart in the day shift, the night cleaner always started her duties in the upper hallways of the main building which seemed to be clear of students the fastest and then she'd moved downstairs by 7:00pm at the latest.

She'd spend a couple hours working in the lower hallways and adjoining classrooms before heading into the library, front office and the gymnasium. Then she'd leave through the door at the end of the main hallway which acted as a thoroughfare nearest the gym, which she conveniently left unlocked during her shift. It seemed as though she had determined coming and going between this door and the one closest to it at the Annex building was the fastest route to follow when cleaning the entire school and, by leaving them unlocked for a short time during her shift, she wouldn't have to fiddle with finding keys while carrying her cleaning supplies.

She'd then speedily progress to the Annex building and tidy up until the last forty-five minutes or so of her shift when she'd return any supplies to the storage room before locking up and leaving. It would be too risky to try and break in to any of the offices downstairs as a few teachers always seemed to stick around late marking and a handful of kids took part in clubs or teams which held practices into the early evening. Despite the traffic downstairs early on, they would have plenty of time between 7:00pm and 11:15pm to gather whatever tests they'd need from the offices in the abandoned upstairs hallway in the main building and the Annex without worry of getting caught. Both Billy and Mark were paid well in weed for their reconnaissance services to Jason.

The team agreed to meet at Jason's house after school one day to work out the details of the plan. They would have to wait until the day or two prior the start of exam week before attempting to steal them, just to be certain that each of the tests would be on hand in the school- there would be no point in risking everything in order to steal only one or two of the tests. Once they'd have the exams in hand, they knew just who to write them ahead of time and once they had the answers, it would be easy enough to memorize them and the rest would be history.

Chapter XXX-

William, Billy, and Nathan hung around the school for a bit making certain that the janitors were sticking to their regular schedule and that no outside clubs or teams had been booked in to use any of the school facilities that night. The use of the facilities such as the library or gymnasium by external clubs was limited, as the school refused to rent out its spaces because of the extra cost required for cleaning and maintenance after user groups had been there.

Once they were adequately convinced that the building was accessible, they darted off to 7-11 to pick up some snacks and drinks which they finished before heading to Jason's place as planned. For a while, the boys had been cautious about coming back into the convenience store under the assumption that Clay would have probably ratted them out for the last beating they had given him and that the employee who had found him that morning would have banned them from the premises. But to their delightful surprise, Clay had said nothing and their crew had kept full access.

Meanwhile, Jason crushed the remainder of a joint he, Mark and Leon had just finished smoking in his room. They knew the day before final exams started that Clay would likely be studying at the library in town. This was something he did before tests during his last year at Pine Creek School. It had worked well for him so, even though Stonebridge's library was perfectly suitable, it was something that he had continued and Jason had taken notice again last semester when he had seen Clay and Dallas there prior to midterm exams.

Jason knew he'd need something to convince Clay to leave the library and come with them. He'd also have to persuade him to answer the test questions honestly once they had them.

It was going to take drastic measures. Threatening to beat him up wouldn't be enough. They had done that to him too many times by now. The fact that Clay had kept his mouth shut after being abused like that had become vital for their current plan- he was about to endure much worse. Jason was certain Clay had kept his silence so many times, that the coward would definitely be too scared to talk after this night was over.

Jason Blithe's father was a hunter during the fall and kept most of his rifles locked in a gun safe in the garage. The guns had always intrigued Jason and he liked the idea of killing things for sport. Those guns secured in the lockbox would be impossible to access, as the only key to the safe was kept on his father's key ring and he was gone for the night. There was another place to find a gun however, and it was his piece anyway.

Jason left his friends in the basement and headed up stairs to his parents' room. He knelt on the floor beside their bed and peered underneath. It was dark but he could make out the rectangular shape of a shoebox. He reached and grasped the far edge of the box with his hand, sliding it towards him and out from under the bed. Taking the lid off the box, he found the old Official Police Issue Colt hand gun that had been left to him when his uncle died.

His uncle had been a cop in the city before he retired and when he passed away he had left the gun to Jason in his will. The Colt, made of fine carbon steel, was manufactured between 1927 and 1969 and it became the standard gun issued to men in service. Because it was a restricted firearm, he was required to possess a valid licence to actually own it himself. His father took the restricted firearm safety course, registered the gun in his own name and agreed to store it until Jason turned eighteen, which he had done earlier this school year.

The only other stipulation was that Jason had to take the course for himself in order to be in possession of the gun or the ammunition, the .38 Special cartridges, a box of which sat there with the pistol. This was something Jason had not yet done for fear of failing the course and it was the reason why his father had retained the gun in the shoebox under his bed.

Jason picked up the gun and the box of cartridges and began filling it with bullets. He had been hunting with his dad enough times to be comfortable loading pretty much any gun and he looked forward to firing it. For now, the safety was left on.

Jason came back down to his room holding the gun in his right hand. His buddies were still there waiting for him.

"Whoa man! Where'd you get that?" Leon's eyes fixed on the light flickering off the steel of the gun.

"My uncle gave it to me," Jason said.

"Is it loaded?"

"Yeah," Jason spoke with a purpose reconfirming he was in charge tonight.

"Are you gonna use it?" Mark asked trying not to sound confrontational.

"I'm just going to scare him with it." Even Jason was unsure how serious he was about using the gun. He had not really stopped to think about actually shooting Clay, but the kid had been under his skin for years and he knew he hated him. Jason tucked the gun under his shirt into the front of his pants where his belt held it firmly in place. The boys headed out and hopped in Mark's truck, driving to Pine Creek Public Library in silence.

"Mark, you stay here in the truck to keep it running. Me and Leon will go and get him," Jason was working hard at steadying himself enough to go through with the plan. There was no way he was going to back out in front of his friends. His credibility with them and his whole future depended on him staying true to the course he had set.

"How are you going to get him to come out?" Mark asked, seeing a potential flaw in the plan.

"Leave that to me," responded Jason. A fast escape would be necessary to ensure Clay wouldn't do anything stupid and call out for help. Mark kept the truck idling against the sidewalk in front of the main entrance to the building. Jason and Leon entered the library. It was nearly empty at this time in the day; the only people there being an elderly lady with a couple of grandchildren in the sectioned off area full of books for young readers and the staff, one of which was busy shelving books near the back of the building while the other manned the circulation desk.

It was a novel place for each of them and it took them a moment to locate Clay. He had found a quiet corner at an individual-sized table behind the stacks of books where he could study in peace. His green backpack had been tossed on the floor next to one of the table legs and a few books were piled around where he was working writing notes in a pad of paper.

Jason and Leon snuck up from behind Clay unnoticed. Taking a position on either side of him, Jason spoke firmly but not loud enough for anyone else to hear, "You need to come with us."

"You're crazy."

"I know you heard me. Now get up and let's go."

"I'm not going anywhere with you. I don't care what you say. If you don't leave me alone..."

Jason cut him off. "What? What are you gonna do?" He held his shirt up enough to show Clay the stock of the gun. Clay's eyes grew wide and his jaw dropped open. Leon was standing there in disbelief while Jason held the bottom of his T-shirt bunched up in his fist, the object unmistakeable in its ferocity clearly evident.

An uncontrolled rush of air released from Clay's lungs and with it went any chance of him calling for help. He sat there speechless. Clay's mind spiralled wildly out of control as he attempted to process what was happening.

"We have your mom and you need to come with us." Jason's voice gave no inclination that he was lying and Clay knew that if he was irrational enough to draw a gun here, he just might be telling the truth. After losing his brother and father, there was no way he was going to lose his mother too.

Clay stood up and followed Jason as he led him out to the truck. Leon grabbed Clay's books and stuffed them into the backpack sitting on the floor, then picked up the bag and followed closely behind the others.

Mark sat in the driver's seat with the window down watching them come out. He expected Clay to look a bit off, but he could tell by the pale look on Leon's face that something serious had just taken place inside.

"Get in and don't say a word," Jason instructed. Clay climbed in the passenger side and Leon and Jason jumped in beside him. Jason took the gun from his pants and held it on the knee of his leg closest to the truck door where Clay could see it. It was a short drive through the sleepy community to Jason's house.

Clay's heart pounded heavy in his chest and he wasn't sure if he had taken a breath since departing the library. His mother was the only thing on his mind.

When they pulled up to the house, Jason opened the door and ushered his prisoner out by pointing the gun towards him and waving it in the direction of the house. Leon went first through the screen door onto the inner landing and then down to the basement and stood by the thick door to Jason's bedroom waiting for it to be unlocked.

Clay followed, attempting a question, "Leon, is my mom OK?"

Leon, still stunned himself, ignored him.

Jason came down, turning to maintain his aim at Clay as he stepped past him on the stairs and then he punched in the code for his lock and pushed open the door. Again, he waved the gun at Clay. "Go inside and sit down."

Clay stepped in partly hoping that his mother wouldn't be there and partly wishing she was standing there unharmed in front of him- at least that way he'd know she was alright. They made their way inside the room still reeking of marijuana smoke.

"Sit down," Leon pointed over to one of the sofa chairs set up in front of the TV.

Clay obliged.

"Where's my mom? What have you done to her?" Clay sat down, puzzled about what was taking place.

"Don't worry. She's not here. She's fine. Just do what we say and you'll be fine." Leon, who was feeling the whole ordeal was going a bit over board, tried to calm down their captive.

"She's gone? Tell me she's alright."

"We never had her." Leon tossed the backpack on the bed and sat beside it. "Just do as he says."

Mark was pacing back and forth by the door mumbling something to himself about how messed up the situation was getting.

Jason had tucked the gun back into his pants and was now opening a closet door and pulling out a long length of what appeared to be climbing rope and a thickly linked bike chain with a key lock attached to one end. He tossed the chain next to the backpack and then proceeded to wrap the rope tightly around both Clay and the chair cinching the cord taut with each loop around him. His arms were pinned at his sides, the rope becoming so tight that it was digging into his skin, rubbing against bone wherever the skin was thinnest. His feet and hands felt as if they were getting cold as the circulation was being reduced to a minimum. Around and around Jason went with the rope, finally tying it off behind the back of the chair out of reach.

Jason spun the chair around so that it was facing the bed. Then he sat down on the corner of the mattress, retrieved the gun from his waist and held it two feet from Clay's face aimed directly at the end of his nose.

Clay knew that many people in Pine Creek hunted and possessed guns, but his parents did not. In fact, Clay had never seen a gun aside from ones on television. All Clay knew about guns was that the one pointed at him had a nickel plated finish with a stock of darkened walnut and two nickel finished Colt medallions on it. It had a six inch barrel to match a six round cylinder and he had to believe it was loaded.

Jason sat there on the end of the bed refusing to lower the gun and explained the essential parts of his plan to Clay. He informed him that they'd be gone for a while and when they returned, the group would have some paperwork he'd have to do for them. He advised Clay that they did not yet have his mother, but that it was something they were willing to do if he didn't cooperate.

Chapter XXXI-

Jason's parents were out playing poker at friend's house and wouldn't be home for the entire evening. Jason paced back and forth in the room on edge from having Clay sitting there and knowing he was in deep and from smoking a joint and chasing it with a couple of energy drinks.

While Clay sat there watching helplessly, Jay picked up Clay's backpack and began sifting through the pockets.

"Look at this ripped up piece of crap bag." In one pocket, he found a few coins and a five dollar note which he promptly stuffed into the pocket of his jeans. In the other, he found Clay's phone. Jay turned it on seeing the stock image of an ocean wave on the home screen.

Nothing special- there wasn't anything special enough in Clay's life to deserve being put on his phone. Jay swiped through the recent phone calls before being quickly distracted by Leon anxiously fumbling around with a model car on the dresser.

"Quit screwing around," Jason ordered. Leon scowled and tossed the car back on the dresser. It slid off, falling behind the back side of the dresser and got wedged between it and the wall. Jason went back to focusing his attention on the phone. An incoming number from one day when Clay's mother had called him was at the top of the recent calls list. Jay selected the number and began typing a message on the screen's tiny keyboard.

douche

He hit SEND on the phone and then snickered as he closed that program and opened a digital folder labelled PHOTOS. There were few photos stored in the phone- no surprise given that he had never saved anything better than the waves on the home screen. It wasn't long before Jason stumbled across the image of Dallas risking it all laying there exposed and shirtless.

"What the hell is this?" Jason's voiced elevated with excitement. "Come check this out, guys!" He held the phone so that the screen pointed towards the others in the room.

Clay turned seeing him waving the device back and forth like a flag. "Give it back!"

"Shut up!" the gun now replacing the phone being waved in Clay's direction.

Clay gritted his teeth. *It's her fault,* he told himself trying to self-reassure and put his conscience at ease. *It's her fault.*

The others gathered around the phone, eyes bulging at the screen shot of Dallas Hilton looking like a Playmate. They took turns making jeers of inappropriate cat calls, each one seeming to try and one up the others by being more foul and misogynistic.

"I've got an idea." Jason said. "Why don't we invite your little girlfriend to this study party?"

The others continued to amuse themselves with the vision of Dallas on the phone, but Clay could tell by the way Jason spoke that he had seriously terrible intentions. *I hate this guy. What is wrong with him?* He clenched his teeth harder not noticing he was pinching the edge of his tongue. The pungent iron taste of blood brought him back to reality. "She's not my girlfriend. She dumped me for you. Remember?"

He hoped Jason would be satisfied with the explanation enough to drop the subject. It was to no avail. Clay felt ashamed that he didn't have the ability or courage to stop them. To the dismay of his friends, who continued to remark about the image, Jason began texting another message; this one in his most sincere and caring tone to Dallas. He'd have to make her believe that it was Clay on the other end of the phone.

I miss u.

Huh?

Dallas's response was almost immediate.

I miss u. Can we talk?

K. miss u 2. where? when?

Jay was beside himself with how dumb she was being and how well his plan was coming together.

10 O'clock? @ your school?

K. C u soon ☺

Jason tucked the phone into the back pocket of his jeans next to his lighter. He was now growing more impatient waiting for the others, Nathan, William and Billy, to arrive when he heard them coming down the stairs leading to the basement. He entered the code into the door lock then swung open the heavy wooden barricade to his room before they reached the bottom of the stairs.

"What took you so long?" he said with a jitter in his voice. "We've been waiting for you and it's already 6:30pm." Mark and Leon were sitting on the edge of his bed playing video games in between taking swigs of some fizzy liquid lightning.

Clay sat tied to the chair where he had been left. The new arrivals took a few seconds to make sense of the situation in the room.

Jason picked up a black hockey bag from near the doorway and yelled at his friends, "Let's go guys."

The group filed out the door which Jason made sure to shut snugly and lock behind them. Clay breathed deeply as he watched the door close. As they arrived at Pine Creek School a few minutes before seven, Jason led the group to a spot in between a couple of portable semi-trailers that had been put on blocks and converted into classrooms when the school's population had grown beyond its walls. He dropped the hockey bag and unzipped it, pulling the contents from within.

"Here. Put these on." He tossed the five other guys a black ski mask to wear. The boys obliged, figuring it would be best not to be seen doing a break and enter. As was common belief among teenagers, they all knew they would be able to outrun any janitor who worked at the school should they be spotted during the heist and counted on being able to make a smooth getaway long before any police officers could be on the scene. "We're sticking together because we'll need to keep watch, but if shit hits the fan, it's everyone for themselves. Just keep your mouth shut if you get caught. Alright?"

With Jason's last command the other boys suddenly realized that there may in fact be a real possibility of getting busted and each snapped his head back and forth eyeing the others looking for reassurance. "Alright?" Jason asked again this time more sternly than the last.

The others agreed, trying to seem confident though not sounding entirely so.

"I've got Clay's phone. Mark and Billy have theirs. Turn your phones on vibrate. We'll use texts to communicate if we need to." Jason took Clay's phone out of his pocket and scrolled through the home screens until he found its number.

Then, the group took a minute to input Clay's cell phone number into their own phones. They each flipped switches or pushed buttons until all of the phones were silenced.

"What time is it now?" asked Nathan.

Billy looked at his phone as he flicked the mute switch on the side of it. "7:01pm."

And with that, the boys made their way around the side of the main building of the school to the doorway between the gymnasium hallway and the Annex. William peeked through the glass panel in the door while the rest stood with their backs up against the cool reddish outer brick wall of the school, looking like some narcotics police squad ready to break into a drug house unannounced. William made sure the coast was clear and then waved the boys through the open door.

There was no one to be seen the entire way down the long hallway. The school seemed eerily quiet, but under the circumstances, this is just what they had hoped for. With a sped up mix of tip toeing and shuffling, the robbers scampered to one of the main staircases leading up to the hallway where the majority of the faculty offices were.

Jason took his role of commander again. "Billy, you have a phone so you and Nathan will work together. You two make your way all the way to the other end of the hallway to the other staircase leading up here." He pointed on an angle up the staircase on which he stood breathing heavily in his mask. "Make sure she doesn't see you," he ordered, referring to the janitor on duty. "She could be in any one of these lower classrooms by now. Text me if you see her and let us know when you get to your spot. Mark will stay here and guard this staircase."

Mark did not seem pleased with having to work alone, but he was obedient.

Billy and Nathan started down the hallway on the main floor in pursuit of the far staircase while the others waited in the cover of where they stood for a text letting them know that the two had arrived safely at their designated position. Both Nathan and Billy were a bit nervous and Nathan, who kept thinking he was hearing the custodian opening doors, had them diving into doorways of various classrooms to find cover. He had sworn on a number of occasions that he could hear her actually turning a class's doorknob and assumed that she'd step out into the concourse and spot them sliding by in their balaclavas.

Billy pushed him along knowing they'd be less likely to get caught if they could just get to where they needed to be. They had advanced approximately a third of the way when Billy gave Nathan a wicked smile as they both acknowledged the wet floor sign outside the door to one of the girls' bathrooms. Knowing she must be head down cleaning a bank of nasty toilets, they quickened their pace down the hall hoping she wouldn't be popping out and heading into the adjacent boys' washroom just as they were passing by. The boys were in luck and all was quiet as they hustled undetected to the far end of the school where the only other major staircase would lead upstairs.

We're here.

Billy's text buzzed in Jason's hand.

"They made it. Mark you stay here. We'll be right back. Remember, text us if you see anything." Jason began to slither up the staircase.

Leon and William bounded up the steps after him as if their clamoring was not making any noise. They arrived at the landing at the top of the stairs and pressed their faces up to the glass door separating the stairwell from the hallway. Each set of eyes looked this way and that but saw nothing.

"Let's go!" Leon whispered with enthusiasm.

William pushed open the double doors which swung silently on their three large hinges and he and Leon squeezed through when they were open just enough to slip between.

Bzzzt. Bzzzt. "Just wait. I got a text." Jason said calling them back. He looked down at the phone in his open palm. His hand shook with adrenaline infused with caffeine and taurine the key stimulants comprising the main ingredients in his beverages of choice.

Hurry up.

"Fuck!" Jason said as he read the message. Billy was getting ancy. "It's nothing. Just Mark, telling us to hurry." He clicked the phone again and put it back in his pocket. "OK, Go! Go! Go!"

The three boys headed down the hallway to the first office door. Mr. Jeffries, the English Teacher, would be the first. They could see into the office space through a large glass window next to the door which was partially covered with posters taped to the inside of the glass. There was a bulky L-shaped desk littered with paper and a black synthetic leather chair on rolling wheels pushed in just where Mr. Jeffries had left it earlier in the day. More importantly, there was a black metal filing cabinet against one of the walls.

That's where it'll be, Jason thought to himself. William tested the door knob with the turn of his wrist. It was securely locked. Jason, skilled in lock picking in his youth, was not about to waste time in the hallway trying to pick open a door when at any moment the janitor could stroll by. They were all too nervous for that and eagerly wanted into the sanctum of the office itself. The group had planned for this moment.

William and Leon moved close beside the door and crossed their forearms before clasping their hands together. As they made a couple of X shapes with their joined arms and tightened the grips between their hands, they formed a steady table. Crouching down, Jason climbed on top of their arms standing tall when they stood upright again. He was now tall enough to reach the low roof of the hallway. Jason flattened his palm on the ceiling tile directly over them and immediately along the roof nearest to the office doorway and pushed it up and to the side creating an opening leading into dark space above. The two boys boosted him further.

William, the taller of the two, allowed Jason to use his shoulder as a final step as he climbed up into the ceiling.

The two boys stood watching Jason disappear into the darkness overhead using the sturdier wall joists near the door frame as supports for his climbing. Moments later, Leon tapped William on the shoulder urging him with an outstretched arm and pointing index finger to look through the window and into the office. White dust flecks fell from the ceiling and landed square on the desk. Then crumbs. Then fingers were visible poking through one of the ceiling tiles. The tile was pulled aside and a pair of legs dropped down onto the desk. Jason was careful not to step on any of the assignments left waiting to be marked on the desk as he hopped onto the seat of the chair followed by the floor. He smiled through the window as he open the office door from the inside letting the other two boys in.

William shut the door behind them and Leon took the place of watchdog looking through the window while Jason extracted two small pieces of metal stuffed next to his lighter in the pocket of his blue jeans. The shiny pieces of straightened paperclips were slid into the keyhole of the filing cabinet and in a matter of seconds the drawer was being slid open.

"Bingo." Jason said as he began flipping through the labeled files in search of the first final exam of the night. He quickly found a folder neatly scribed with the word FINAL on the tab at the top and from the back he took a stapled booklet entitled: Pine Creek Community High School- English 12 Final Exam. This one they'd need for tomorrow.

Jason snatched it up and pulled out Clay's phone. He switched the phone over to the camera setting and snapped a photograph of each page as he leafed through the test. The crystal clear images were saved in the phone's digital album. Jason slid the test back into the folder and made sure to place it exactly as it had been found in the filing cabinet. They expertly replaced the missing ceiling tile above the desk and put any misplaced papers and the desk chair back to their original positions before leaving through the office door which they promptly locked. William put the hallway tile back and they moved on toward the next office.

Mark stood watching carefully downstairs. He couldn't see the entire length of the hallway and therefore, could not see his other friends standing guard. What he did see was the janitor opening the bathroom door partway down the hall.

She held the end of a long dripping wet mop and stuffed it into the top of a mop bucket which she then pushed a few feet further. She let go of the mop and bent to move the sign indicating her work was now going to be "in progress" in the boys' washroom next door.

Mark thought he could just make out the fact that she was wearing earphones before she disappeared into the bathroom. He texted Billy and Jason:

She just went in the boys' washroom part way down the hall. We have some time, but hurry up!!!!

Billy and Nathan were relieved when they read the message. Leon, Jason and William were too busy to celebrate just yet. They were just about to repeat their operation on the second office belonging to Miss Johnson, the mathematics teacher.

The three teens arrived at her office ready to steal her version of the math 12 final. Again, they boosted Jason through the white tiles of the ceiling where he could make his way over the wall separating them from their treasure within the sealed room.

This time, as he inched forward in the blackness, he had to avoid the sprinkler system and some ventilation ducts as he passed over the wall. The metal beams on which he was perched were cool under his hands. A thick layer of dust covered the four inch wide lengths of steel. As he tried to crawl along the narrow beams past a large, hollow, metal pipe in the darkness of the roof, he was forced to stretch with his arm to grasp a girder just out of reach. His hand slid off the dusty beam directly onto one of the fragile tiles, punching through and breaking the tile in half. Jason let out a muffled yelp as he held strong with his other hand on a neighboring beam, his knees bruising from the unforgiving steel below them and his hip backed into the ventilation duct making a hollow drumming sound that echoed down the pipe.

Leon and William heard the noise but were too afraid to call out to see if he was OK. Jason steadied himself enough to pull his hand back into the darkness and put it against the duct, muting the sound which vibrated the metal tube. Then, he turned his body so that he could drop down into the office through the new hole he had

185

created where the broken tile had once been. Once inside, he brushed the broken pieces of tile off of his shirt and opened the office door so that Leon and William could enter.

"You OK?" questioned William.

"What was all that noise?" Leon asked.

"Don't worry about it. I just broke a tile." Jason seemed calmer than he should have been as he brushed the remaining dust particles from his pants. "I'll find the test while you guys look for some tape to fix it."

"But Johnson will see it," chirped Leon.

"Tape up the back of it. She might see the crack but this old building is falling apart anyway. She'll likely think it was a just mouse or something," Jason did his best to stop the others from worrying about something they no longer could control. "We just have to hurry and hope the cleaner didn't hear us."

Jason spotted the math test sitting face down on the edge of the teacher's desk. Although it should have been securely locked away, the boys were pleased with Miss Johnson's lack of skepticism regarding the exam's safety. She must have simply set it there on the table in eagerness to photocopy it for her classes early the following morning.

Downstairs, Mark was watching the janitor mopping her way out the door of the boys' washroom. She continued swiping the mop back and forth as if it was her dancing partner just outside the entrance when she paused to fiddle with her earphones. Mark had heard the dull bang of metal from the boys upstairs. Obviously, she had not. Instead, she had been getting into one of the songs playing loudly through the mp3 player attached to her waist. Assuming she was alone in the building, she had begun to sing the chorus lines with vigor; occasionally wailing in some unknown language loud enough that Mark could hear her clearly but still not figure out what the racket was she was listening to.

Whatz up? we heard something.

The text from Billy's phone arrived simultaneously to Mark's and Clay's, which Jason held firmly.

We r good here. She's mopping down the hallway. It will take her a while and she can't hear anything. Playing music.

Mark replied to all recipients. Billy read the thread and shared the news with Nathan who was now sitting bored on the stairs.

Just got 2nd test. 1 more, then Annex.

Jason finished taking pictures of the math exam. The broken tile had been repaired; noticeable, but put back together well enough that it stayed in place above Miss Johnson's desk.

Leon got bold, "If we're stealing all these tests anyway, I want the Calculus one too."

"It's not even until later in the week," William said.

"It's right next door and I want it. I can't study for that stuff," Leon persisted.

"Fine. Come on." Jason settled their argument in an instant while closing the filing cabinet and ushering the other boys out the door. Mr. Griffin's calculus test was a quick snatch anyway. It was like he had knowingly placed his filing cabinet right under where Jason could easily step down from the roof. He had also left it unlocked and the clearly labeled test was one of only a couple of booklets inside. Several high definition pictures were quickly stored in the phone's digital memory.

The three could hardly hold back their laughter as they sped out of the last office carrying the images of English, calculus and math finals on the phone and headed down the hall to the stairs where Mark patiently waited to meet up with them.

They needed to get into the top floor of the Annex next. That's where the biology test would be. Jason fired off a text from Clay's phone telling Billy and Nathan to head out the nearest door without being seen and to come around the outside of the school to meet up with Mark and his group by the Annex doors. Mark joined the three boys as they came down the staircase and moved outside to the covered walkway leading to the Annex building. Within seconds Billy and Nathan arrived out of breath.

"Did you get 'em?" Nathan asked through the moisture soaked mouth hole of his mask.

"Yeah. Piece of cake. We even got my calculus test," said Leon proud of their acquisitions thus far.

"We have to hurry. We don't have all night. We still have to convince our good friend to give us the answers." Jason remembered that Clay, likely worried and exhausted, had been waiting at the house for almost an hour and a half. He would certainly need some encouragement to write the tests and Jason was very much looking forward to giving it to him.

They all took off their masks and held them in their hands as they walked briskly, each with their own swagger, across the walkway separating the Annex and main school complex. They didn't really want to be spotted wearing the masks roaming around the school yard, but none of the boys needed to be reminded to put them back on as they arrived at the Annex. The doors were unlocked as they had been advised by the scouting report.

"This will be even easier than the last. There's no one even in here," William said.

"Nobody ever comes in here," Nathan joked.

"Maybe we should try and get every test- not just these ones?" Billy asked, feeling he should be part of the conversation. "We could sell them to other kids."

"We don't have time for that. And besides, it's too risky," answered Mark.

"Yeah, and we don't want everyone getting good marks on these tests or they might end up grading on the curve," said Jason.

Nathan weighed in, "And I want to be at the top of the class for once."

"As if that could every happen," Billy chuckled.

"Let's just get out of here." Jason kept them on track. They took the first set of stairs to the upper floor and strolled down to biology teacher's office that used to belong to Mr. Kent before he retired.

The lockers in this hallway were in serious need of repair. Most were severely dented and they all were in desperate need of a fresh coat of paint. The banks of lockers stood about five and half feet tall reaching just high enough for them to stand on to get up into the ceiling. As Mark started boosting Billy on top of the lockers next to the biology professor's door, the others stood waiting close by.

Leon stood intently staring at the door. Suddenly, he turned his head while his eyes glanced upwards and to the side. The whites of his eyes stood out against the black material of the ski mask, making it obvious he was deep in thought. "Hey, this is the old guy's office we used to take stuff from last year. Remember, that guy who retired? We used to steal his pencil sharpener and stapler and hide them on him." Leon was keen to bring up past memories.

"Didn't we steal his doorknob once too?" Billy said looking down from atop the lockers; an exit sign and a small chunk of black electronic equipment that looked like a smoke alarm hung just behind his head.

"Yeah, we took all kinds of his shit- made that old guy crazy. Probably why he retired," Nathan gave a snicker to himself.

"Oh yeah, we just took the thing right off." Mark too, remembered being in on the doorknob shenanigans. "They put it on backwards again." Obviously the janitors who were asked to re-install the doorknob after it had been removed the first time had no idea what they were doing either.

Billy hopped back down from the locker and pulled a red multi-tool knife from his pocket. He lifted the ski mask up over his face and rolled it onto his forehead so that he could have a better time seeing what he was doing. "Might as well go through the door instead of breaking another tile," he said. The others stood aside while Billy used his finger nail to pull a small screw driver from the knife and took hold of the knob. It took all of thirty seconds for him to take out the two screws holding the handle in place, the brassy knob coming off in his palm. He could see the door lock mechanism inside and twisted a square shaped bolt which in turn, retracted the deadbolt from within the door frame. "Simple." Billy said smugly as he pushed the door open. The others could just make out the grin stretching from seam to seam across the mask's mouth hole.

Jason stepped into the office and began looking around. William and Leon watched the hallway from either side of the door, while Mark and Nathan followed Jason inside to search for the exam.

The teacher that had taken over this space had been a new one on probation and had done little to decorate the room.

There were no pictures of family or friends, posters or signs, nor were there many papers sitting on the desk or projects waiting to be marked. There wasn't even a filing cabinet in the room. Mr. Kent must have taken it with him or some other teacher reallocated it to their classroom when Kent's unwanted stuff went up for grabs after he left. Perhaps he hadn't intended on staying at the dismal Pine Creek High School too long. It was equally likely that he wasn't a good enough teacher to be kept on a permanent contract anyway. It was the end of the year after all and several teachers became part of the regular attrition that happened each June.

The only thing left on the wall was a clock which read 8:12pm. They needed to be quick as there was much work for Clay to do when they would return. Mark had stepped back into the doorway to help Billy start reassembling the door knob.

"Found it." Nathan blurted out as he was in the process of sifting through some papers on the edge of the desk. Leon snatched it from his hands and handed it to Jason. Jason took off his mask and retrieved the camera from the pocket of his jeans. He gave the test a once over and commented on how hard it looked.

"There's no way I could have passed this class. I don't know any of this," he said. Given that he was the mastermind of his crew, it left little doubt in any of the others' minds that they too would have had difficulty mustering even a passing grade in biology class without seeing the exam beforehand.

Jason once again snapped photos of each of the pages before putting it back into the pile of papers on the desk where it had been found. "Let's get outta here." The boys shut the door behind themselves and Billy tightened the screws, checking to see that the door was locked and that the doorknob was secure. William and Leon let them know there was no sight of anyone else and they took off in a short sprint along the hallway, down the stairs and out the Annex door. The teens slipped away from the building, but not before Jason took a moment to stop by the portables in order to grab his hockey bag as they bolted through the crisp night air.

Chapter XXXII-

The crew arrived at Jason's basement suite at approximately 8:30pm. The sun was finally starting to drop below the mountains and the room, which had a few windows all covered in dark curtains, struggled to let any light in. It was shadowy and ominous in the bedroom even after Billy flicked a switch and brought a lamp next to the bed to life. Jason had just over an hour before he'd have to head back to meet Dallas. Looking over at Clay, who was sitting frightened in the chair just as they had left him, he decided he better get his little slave to work.

Jason walked over to the chair where Clay was sitting and reminded him of the Colt pistol he'd been carrying all evening by withdrawing it from his waistband and flashing it in front of his prisoner. "Now you're gonna do as we say or somebody is getting hurt. Could be you. Could be your mom. Could even be your girlfriend. You probably know how rough she likes it."

The nickel finish looked slightly golden as it reflected the incandescent light of the lamp. Clay hadn't had a girlfriend in some time but he knew exactly who was being referred to. Fear had taken a hold of him even more tightly than the rope still binding him to the seat.

The other boys in the room stood behind Jay forming a semi-circle around their prisoner as he nodded his head in agreement. Billy picked up the chain and lock that was still sitting on the bed and used it to fasten Clay's legs together and then link them to the metal frame of the bed nearby. He began to loosen the ropes from Clay's chest by sliding them down, eventually exposing and freeing his arms which were red from the overly abrasive nature of the threads.

Jason drew Clay's phone from his pocket, switched the power back on, and turned the screen so that it faced the incarcerated boy. The photos showing the test pages turned out crystal clear on the screen and Clay's mind began struggling to piece together what possible events must have occurred in order for them to have taken the images.

"Now here's the plan. We need you to give us the answers to these tests. As soon as that happens, we can let you go. As long as you keep your mouth shut, which we know you will, you'll never have us bother you again." Jason's words were a mixture of commands and deceptions, neither of which surprised the boy still fixating on his phone being held slightly out of reach in front of him.

"Where did you get those?" Clay asked.

"Never mind. Do you understand what we are telling you to do?" Jason was visibly getting agitated. They could all hear the tenacity in his voice. Apparently he was used to his friends taking orders a bit more promptly and without question. "And you can't say anything or you're dead." Jason's argument was strong. Not once had Clay, who was deathly afraid of the consequences, ever ratted them out before and Jason was counting on this being the case again. The shimmer of the gun in his hand dutifully provided strength to his demands.

"Yeah. I guess." Clay was feeling all out of options. "How many questions are there?"

"There are three tests."

Clay jerked his head back, equally shocked at the audacity and the ability of the group for stealing so many assessment papers without getting caught.

"Four," Leon spoke up making sure his calculus test wouldn't be left out.

Jason turned his head and eyeballed Leon who returned the favor. "We'll start with three and see how long it takes. The calculus one isn't important." He turned back towards Clay, "And it better not take long. We still have to memorize this shit before tomorrow."

Some of the boys in the room were expecting that task to be the most difficult of the night. A couple of them even wondered if they shouldn't be making cheat sheets with the answers to help them avoid the difficulty of memorizing.

"Grab that table," Jason gestured at Billy standing near the lamp who promptly dragged the table in front of Clay. "What else do you need?"

"Some paper... I guess. And... something to write with? And maybe a calculator depending on what exams they are."

"Here's some paper and a pen but you're shit outta luck for a calculator in this place," Leon said handing him a pen and a pad with several sheets of lined paper. Jason turned the phone to airplane mode to limit access to incoming and outgoing calls and messages and then swiped through the screens to find the first page of the English exam. He then casually set the phone down in front of Clay on the table. "Use the calculator on the phone," Jason barked. "But nothing else."

Clay, feeling anxious, started writing as the delinquents in the room took turns watching him intently making sure he didn't try and call out using the phone. When not on shift they either passed the time smoking up or drinking beers stolen from the Blithe's fridge upstairs. Jason was never far away and kept the gun in his hand, at times waving it around pretending to shoot at something. Every once and a while, Jason would point the barrel toward Clay; only making it harder for him to focus on what he was trying to write.

While Clay busily wrote the exam answers for each test he began to feel that by now all was lost. If he didn't do as Jason's gang wished they'd likely kill him. *They had gone too far now to turn back,* he thought to himself. He glanced over and looked at Jay standing holding the gun aimed directly at the temple on the left side of his own head.

Clay wasn't much for a religious person- certainly not after the death of his brother. So, thinking of the possibility of being shot and there being an afterlife was not something of solace for him. He was not about to die over some tests. *Besides*, he could see Jason standing there with a tyrannous look in his eyes. *This was the look of a kid with literally nothing to lose.*

He had lost his girlfriend and wasn't likely to get another any time soon. He had been failing out of school. His family life was the pits. He had been physically injured enough to be stripped of sure-thing scholarships. He had physically abused Clay enough times that Clay knew he was serious about harming him and, now that Jason had brought a deadly weapon into the mix, he seemed all the more likely to use it. If Clay didn't write the correct answers and Jay and the others ended up failing this exam, they would surely come after him or even his mother or Dallas as they had promised.

Seconds seemed to tick by as if time were stuck at a red light. Clay kept writing. The questions were easier than he had expected them to be and he filled the papers with ink making sure the words were clear and legible so as to not piss off anyone who may have difficulty with reading. The English and math tests were now finished.

Jason continued to focus his attention on using the gun to convince Clay to write faster. "Hurry up- I have a date with your girlfriend," he mocked.

Clay wasn't sure exactly what had been sent to Dallas through his phone earlier in the evening but he figured she would be getting involved in this mess somehow very soon. He tried to play through different scenarios in his head. *Could he escape? Could he somehow get a hold of someone for help? Maybe Dallas? No... He did not want to get her involved any more than she may already be.* Should Dallas arrive after he was finished with the tests, he hoped he would be able to keep their attention on him instead.

He thought about stalling as he worked on the biology test, pretending not to know the answers to some of the questions and needing time to think them through, calculate, or to cross out responses and rewrite them, hoping that if she did show up at the basement, he'd still be here.

Woomp! A dull thump to the temple by Leon's fist made him reassess his strategy as he shook off the blurred vision that resulted shortly after impact. He tried to refocus on writing appropriate answers to the questions while at the same time noticing Jay had headed into the bathroom.

"Don't get any funny ideas," Leon bellowed. Mark followed suit with a smack from the palm of his hand on the back of Clay's head in a way that solidified his place as one of the hired muscles in the room. Compared to the punch he had just endured, the slap was hardly noticeable.

Clay got back to his work. The washroom door opened and Jason stepped out looking down at the table and the evidence of progress that had been made on the exams thus far. He turned to Mark and whispered something in his ear. It was too quiet for Clay to make out. "I've gotta go meet Dallas. You guys get him to finish up, and then take him to our party spot in the woods."

Mark tipped his head up and raised his eyebrows.

"Bring the chain."

Mark smiled wickedly indicating he understood the plan.

Jason tucked the gun into the front of his pants and then shuffled through his dresser picking out a grey hoodie screened with the logo of a team from the National Hockey League.

"Shut the door behind you," he said as he pulled on the hoodie so that the hood stayed covering his head while he left the basement.

Chapter XXXIII-

Jay's walk to Pine Creek School was cold and quiet. The streets were empty as he walked alone and many of the street lights above him seemed to be blown out making the town darker than normal. He strode confidently down the sidewalk knowing he was now deeply involved with something so corrupt that he could be in severe trouble if he ever got caught. He grew excited by the thought. Even his friends had the potential to slip up at some point. *What if they say something to someone?* Jason thought to himself as he walked on in the darkness. *Billy is dumb enough to brag to someone. I'm going to have to do something to make sure even they are too scared to talk.* A sinister grin stretched across his thin lips making the scar on his cheek ripple.

Jason could see Dallas standing against the side of the school behind a bike rack near the front doors. She was leaning with her shoulders against the wall and her head down causing her long hair to drape over her face like a curtain. As he got close enough for her to hear his footsteps on the cement of the sidewalk, she raised her head.

Dallas, expecting to see Clay's slight build coming towards her in the shadows, lifted her head and instantly realized the figure was too large and walking with too confident a gate to be him. She squinted trying to decipher who was approaching. The boldness of his posture and the swagger gave it away.

"Jay?" Dallas questioned rhetorically.

"Hey Dallas," he said getting close enough now for her to make out the angular features of his face and the roughness of his disfigured ear as he pulled off his hood. His slyness made her uneasy as he stepped up to the bike rack and stood in front of her. Though the metal rack separated them, she felt cornered and pushed off the wall to stand upright. Subconsciously, she was scanning around with her eyes behind her bangs for an exit route in the shadows.

"What are you doing here?" she said.

"Why don't we go for a walk? I have something I want to talk to you about." He could tell she was nervous by the way her eyes seemed to be looking around for help from someone. She started moving laterally so that her back was turned and no longer facing the wall of the school. Jay leaned up against the rack so that he was only a few feet away. He decided to try another tactic. "He's not coming."

"What?" Dallas's head cocked slightly to the side and her eyes now fixed on his.

"He's not coming, I said."

"Who?" Dallas tried hard to keep her comments short.

"You know who... Clay... He's not coming. He saw me walking over here and that chicken shit took off. He's not coming."

Dallas's heart began to sink and she wondered if she should run but her nerves held her frozen in place. The bike rack between them no longer seemed to provide any shelter.

"Let's go for a walk. I want to talk to you about us." Jason started to pace the length of the bike rack turning around its corner so that he was now against the wall of the school.

"There is no us," Dallas said with a hint of defiance starting to walk the opposite way in a circular motion around the rack in order to keep it between them. She had a clear path across the lawn in front of the school yard to the road. The girl looked down the street, but no cars were in sight. She thought about running but hesitated for just a second too long.

"Come on… I just want to talk." He stopped and stood eying her up and down. She looked like a frightened rabbit behind her brown hair and he could tell she was ready to flee. "I miss you. Can we talk?"

The last two phrases caught her attention. She remembered the text from Clay that brought her here. *"I miss you. Can we talk?" Those were the words Clay used.* She knew something was up and began to move, half walking and half running, so that it became obvious she was alarmed and trying to escape. She took no more than three steps before Jason had stepped around the bike rack and pounced in front of her. He grabbed her by the front of her shirt. Dallas stopped, trembling as he held her by bunching her shirt in his fists which pressed firmly against her collar bone.

"Let me go!" Dallas yelled. Jason let go with one hand and lifted the front of his hoodie. Dallas looked down and could see the handle of the gun against his stomach. She tried to scream again but this time her nerves worked to silence her voice.

"Let's go talk." Jason spun her around so that she stood facing the forest by the school then drew the gun from his waist and pushed it into the small of her back. She could feel the poke of the metal pressing against her spine. Dallas started walking towards the stillness of the trees. The cool and hard steel jabbed into her skin through the thinness of her shirt.

The two figures headed into the old growth of the forest. The trees loomed over her as she marched down the trail system snaking through the brush, ordered by the young man who seemed both wild with his demands to hurry and powerful as he pushed her along. The moss on the side of the trail was dry and witches hair hung from the evergreen branches. The smell of the forest had changed- it was no longer inviting. Now it was terrifying in its cold freshness. She stumbled on the roots that reached out from below her feet tripping her up.

There is no mercy available tonight, he thought.

"Quit screwing around," he ordered picking her up as she stumbled and pushing her along.

Dallas looked down the various small trails leading off from the main path hoping someone else who may be scurrying around in the forest would come across them and offer her some help. *Maybe I could out run him down one of these trails?* The branches seemed to close off all other routes as they passed. Given that exams were taking place the next morning, students would likely all be at home by now cramming or sleeping. *There's no help coming,* she thought.

Maybe someone will be partying out here tonight? Dallas thought desperately but she knew the chances were slim.

When they arrived at the clearing where students often partied, there were in fact people there. For a second she seemed relieved and let out a sigh.

"Help!" she called out.

"They're here," was the response returned by a voice in the shadows. She knew immediately that matters had just gotten worse when she recognized the instability of Billy's jittery voice.

Billy, Mark, Nathan, William and Leon were all there. So was Clay. Jason and Dallas could both tell that the other boys had roughed Clay up a bit more getting him to where he sat near the fire pit by the creek.

He sat there on the rocks hunched over holding his stomach and rocking back and forth. His hair was tussled and his face darkened by what appeared to be either bruising or dirt; likely a combination thereof. Mark and Nathan stood talking quietly together in the trees nearby, while Billy, Leon, and William stood casually gathered around Clay.

Dallas caught a glimpse of a large linked chain being held in one of William's hands and a tattered backpack in the other. Clay had his back to her as Jason nudged her toward the others. Even when Clay heard her whimper, he had little energy to turn around.

"Too many people come through here," Jason started to proclaim to his friends who stopped their own conversations and listened for further instructions.

Dallas and Clay knew otherwise. They wished for it to be true, but both were fully aware how utterly alone they were in the woods with the gang of boys surrounding them; one of them brandishing a gun.

"Let's go off over there just in case somebody comes along." Jason used his chin to point in a direction along a narrow path near the creek and then started ushering Dallas with the gun in her back.

Both captives realized that if Jason was looking for more privacy, things were becoming even more critical. The other boys hooked their arms under Clay's armpits and lifted him to his feet. He moaned a little as he stood and started limping behind Jason and Dallas. The smoothed rocks, wet with mist from the creek, made it more difficult for him but he gradually hopped along wincing with each step.

Eventually they came upon the small area where Dallas had led Clay once before- the day she held his hand for the first time. The day she kissed him for the first time. The day she had the courage to show him her place of solitude. It all happened here in this quiet spot, hidden away in the depths of the forest, in this small town, where no one would hear or see them.

Jason stood there holding Dallas hostage while the boys, still coming down the trail behind them, taunted Clay and gave him shoves from behind in the middle of his back and on his shoulders. Leon pushed him hard as they stepped into the clearing. Clay's back folded like a crescent, the momentum causing him to fall forward against the large fallen log where he and Dallas had sat together more than a year ago. He put out his hands bracing himself as he fell, stopping in a position which made it appear as if he was doing a push up against the log. Clay noticed the initials carved in the wood in front of him. This time, the scratches looked fairly fresh.

DH + CM

Clay stared at the letters dug into the grains of the fir tree and at once understood their significance. Dallas must have carved them proclaiming her love for him. He lowered himself and draped the front of his body against the log. Leon walked over and stood above him, looking down at his broken target, and kicked him once hard in the back of the legs. As he stared at the limp body who hardly stirred with the kick, he too noticed the scratches in the wood. Leon also understood their significance.

"Hey Jason. Get a load of this."

"What?" he replied.

"Look at what's carved into the log. You know who that is?" Leon stepped aside enough so that Jason could view the markings. "It's these two. Looks like they're in love."

"Whatever, idiot!" Jason snapped.

"Who else could it be then?" questioned Mark as he attempted to step in close enough to see for himself. Jason shoved Mark aside and peered down at the log. It took a moment for him to focus on the letters cut in the grain of the wood and to make the connection between Dallas and Clay, but once it registered, something clicked in him. Little noise was made other than the sound of Clay's head bouncing off the log.

Jason held the gun in one hand, and like a wild man, he grabbed Clay by the back of the hair with his other hand and smashed his face forward into the solid wood. The first hit hurt enough for Clay to ignore the second, which stunned him completely and caused him to black out and slip off the front of the log onto the soil. Jason stormed over across the forest floor and grabbed Dallas by the hair, yanking her hard and bending her head toward his waist. She clawed at his hands trying to free them from their entanglement in her hair but he shook her head hard to make her stop. The gun in his opposite hand waved around in the air as the boys watched worryingly that it might accidentally go off in their direction.

"You guys get out of here!" Jason screamed. It was obvious how furious he had become. The rage in him was blowing up like dynamite and even the other boys backed away, fearful for getting caught up in what was about to happen. "I'll deal with these two. Go! I said get out of here!" He yelled the words as if saying them louder made them more meaningful. "I'll meet you back at my place."

Sheepishly, Leon turned and grabbed William. "Come on. Let's go," Leon said. William concurred and turned as if to walk away from the scene before pausing for a moment and saying, "This is getting crazy. I can't be here for this." Then he shook his head back and forth and tossed the back pack and chain at the foot of a tree beside where he had been standing. Leon and William both left along the narrow pathway dropping their heads in shame. The others followed suit and took off down the trail leaving Jason standing there breathing heavily and holding Dallas by the hair while Clay lay motionless near the log. The boys darted off into the darkness heading back to Jason's house where they would spend the remainder of the night memorizing the answers Clay had left for the final exams taking place the following morning.

Jason waited until the sounds of mumbles and footsteps breaking twigs were carried away in the wind and he had caught his breath. He was now standing there calmly calculating his next move. He saw the chain and lock that William had thrown by the tree and quickly came up with an idea. Still holding Dallas by the hair, he pulled her over to the log and, pointing the gun at her face, instructed her to sit down. She sat down with Clay who was just starting to move at her feet.

"Don't fuckin' move." Jason moved the old gun to her mouth and pushed the barrel against her lips, prying them apart so that the metal scraped against her teeth. Then he bent down and took Clay by the wrist. The dark figure dragged the semiconscious victim by the arm away from the fallen log and over to the tree near where William had dropped the back pack and the chain.

Clay squirmed a little as he came to, groaning and holding his forehead and cheek. Blurred outlines of the trees' shadows intermingled with the form of his captor. Jason ordered him to stand up. It took a few seconds, but Clay started to stir. He steadied himself on the ground until his head stopped spinning then stood and brushed the fir needles from his face. Jay picked up the chain and, pinning Clay with his back against the tree and his heels near its base, wrapped it around his captive's torso a couple of times before using the remaining length to secure his hands behind the tree's grand furrowed trunk. The pad lock clicked as he clamped it shut so that it held Clay snugly in place against the bark.

"There you go, Tree Hugger. How do you like that?" Jason muttered condescendingly. "I'm going to leave you here. You know that right? You can stay here all night AND miss your exams tomorrow for all I care."

Clay, now clear of the cobwebs and the blurred vision, could see Dallas sitting on the log facing him. He could also see Jason pacing back and forth in front of him holding the Colt with a vice-like grip so that his knuckles whitened. He pulled at his arms and felt the steel of the chains digging into his wrists behind the trunk. Clay tugged harder, wriggling up and down with his shoulders trying to loosen the chains. It was to no avail. The barked rubbed off the tree behind him, but the chain did not budge. Though he could not see it holding his hands on the opposite side of the trunk, he could feel the pad lock clasped shut with his fingers. Clay stood there bound with scars inside and out to show each of the night's events which had led to that moment. He could no longer watch what was being done and began screaming for help.

"Help us! Helpppp! Pleeeease," he pleaded. "Anybody?"

He listened for anyone to return his calls. The stillness of the chilling spring air combined with the security of the chains made

Clay realize he would never escape the moment. The rippling of the water in the creek seamed to wash away his calls along with any chance of help coming for them. He looked over at Dallas. The moonlight stretching from beyond the crowns of the trees highlighted the fear on her face. She appeared as a stranger that somehow he knew. Her hair was messy and hanging over her face, but there was no confidence in her- not like the first day he saw her in the stairwell at school. Her eyes were now more shaded than the forest around them.

"Shut up or I'll shoot her and then you." Jason punched Clay low in his stomach. "Do you understand me?"

Clay continued rebelliously. "Helppppp! Somebody!"

Jason grew angrier again. Calmly, he took his time to stuff the Colt into the back of his pants securely by his belt, then, in an instant, he exploded and stepped into a heavy punch to Clay's midsection. Clutching both sides of Clay's head with broad, battle scarred hands, Jason slammed him against the tree. His limp body toppled over only to be lifted again so that a second and third punch could be landed to the stomach and torso; the latter catching a couple of the smaller ribs on his side and cracking them with force. Sounds of ribs splintering blended in well with the creaking of the forest.

Jay treaded back a little and unzipped his pants. Pulling down the front of his boxer shorts, he began to urinate on Clay's shoes. He moved forward remaining just out of reach, Clay kicking at him feverishly, and began swaying back and forth covering Clay's trousers with urine. The warmth of the liquid steamed on Clay's jeans in the brisk air.

"William was right. You are crazy," Clay said with a disgusted look on his face.

Standing brazenly with his pants undone, Jason said, "You think that was crazy? How about now you watch me and your girlfriend make out? That'll be fun, hey Dallas?" He strode over to her on the log. "Yeah, that'll be fun." Jason chuckled to himself evilly. "Clay," he whispered, enjoying every second of his prisoner's torment, "remember, you need to keep your mouth shut about this. I'm going to make this the best night of her life." Jay looked down at Dallas draped helplessly over the log.

"You wouldn't," Clay said.

"You can't stop me. Just watch and enjoy the show." Jason reached down and once again wrenched Dallas' head back by her hair.

"No. Don't touch her. What the hell is wrong with you?" Clay struggled with the chains again but could still not free his hands.

Chapter XXXIV-

The next few minutes were more than horrific. Clay yelled the whole way through. But no one heard. No one came running. No one freed him from his chains so that he could stop Jay from raping Dallas in front of him.

Dallas was strong. She put up a fight… for a while. And she yelled too, even while he threatened her with the gun- at least at first. Once she realized that no one was coming to save her and Clay was unable to break the chains no matter how much he wished he could, she just laid there in the dirt and fir needles staring off into the darkness. She had fixed her gaze on the markings she had carved into the log and drifted off into her place of solace until Jay had finished.

Jay had even taken the time to humiliate her further by using Clay's cellular phone to snap a photo of Dallas's half-naked body lying there in the dirt, which he promptly emailed to himself before smashing the device on a rock by the creek. Then, long after Jay had jogged off into the trees and after Clay had stopped asking if she was alright, she got up, mortified and ashamed, and went home. Dallas left Clay chained to the tree. She had been so utterly traumatized by the experience that she had become completely unaware of her surroundings and that, as she left in the darkness, she had been unable to even look at Clay or help to pull him off of the tree to which he was bound.

Chapter XXXV-

The blackness of the trail system winding through the gnarled branches of the thick forest could not hide Clay from any embarrassment or shame he felt tied there against the tree for the past couple of hours. There was no need to hide. No one else was around and no one was coming for him. He could feel the sharpness of the dark and his hands and feet were beginning to numb. His pink nose had started to run and his sniffles were all that broke the silence. The chains pinched the skin on his wrists too.

He was bitter cold and bitter that Dallas had left him; though he knew what she had gone through must have been horrendous. He became a little angry with himself for blaming her and his mind started to wander as he grew tired. Leaning his head back against the tree, Clay thought of the relationship he had had with Dallas over the past couple of years. She really had been the only girl who had given him the time of day and inside he understood that it likely helped him to develop even the small amount of self-respect that he had. His eyes were weary and he was fighting the urge to nod off standing against the tree.

The cool air and the emotional roller coaster caused by the stress of the night's trials had taken their toll and robbed him of his energy. As his head started to bob forward and his eyes started to close, he noticed the back pack sitting near his feet. The shredded bag held together by merely a kilt pin contained little to offer in the way of warmth. He stared at the bag, examining it and wondering if he could drag it close enough to wrap his cold feet in it. As he hooked one of the shoulder straps with his left foot and dragged the bag closer, he noticed the pin once more.

A Pin! Maybe I can pick the lock? Clay snapped alert and felt a glimmer of hope. He pulled the bag closer with his foot so that it rested against the trunk of the tree. Then he spun, pivoting around the tree trunk, rubbing bark off with the chains binding him, and dropped down so that he was sitting at the base of the wooden prison to which he was tied.

Unable to see what he was doing, he used his hands to feel for the kilt pin that had been used to hold the two sides of the bag together when the zipper had broken. Clay grasped the pin and unfastened it. His fingers were stiff and numb but he felt for the needle-like point against his thumb and index finger. Then, he pried it open doing his best to straighten it, fashioning into a tool that he thought might do the trick. With one hand he held the sharp device while he used his other hand to grasp the lock fastening the chains. It took him a few tries to insert the pointed metal into the keyhole on the lock. Fishing around in the hole, he half expected the lock to just pop open magically.

But it was to no avail. Clay picked away at the lock. Blood pooled under his fingernails as they bent back; the cold steel of the lock and the early morning air dulling the pain so that it was no longer noticeable.

This wishful thinking and dextrous work lasted for roughly an hour, during which he paused every so often to contemplate giving up.

The mixture of frustration towards himself, anger at Jason, worry for Dallas and for his mom who by now would have expected him home, drove him each time to continue. Eventually, his calculating mind started to try and understand the object he was working with. He thought about any images of old locks he had seen in the past. All that came to mind were the combination locks kids used for their school lockers and those seemed very different from the one holding him fast. Behind his back, the metal object may as well have been invisible but he used his sense of touch to try and understand how the device worked. It seemed as though he needed something else to hold tension turning the keyhole while he picked away at the tumbler inside.

"Maybe I need something else? But what else can I use?" He thought to himself. *Maybe there's something else in my bag.* Careful not to drop or poke himself with the kilt pin, Clay reached around until he found his bag again behind him in the darkness. It was hanging open and filled with a mixture of books, papers and school supplies. His hand reached in and swiftly darted back and forth feeling for anything of use.

Maybe a pen? He felt several pencils and metal ball point pens at the bottom of his bag and selected one, drawing it out of the pouch. Pushing the tip of the pen into the keyhole, he applied a small amount of pressure as if turning a real key designed for this particular lock. Then he slid the prick of the pin in alongside of the pen as far as it would go into the hole. It was awkward in his hands and he fumbled with the objects, cursing himself as the pen dropped onto the forest floor.

Not giving up hope, Clay reached around in the forest litter until he found the pen again and tried to repeat the set up. It was extremely difficult and this time he took extra caution not to drop anything even though his fingers, which were white at the tips and turning bluish at the knuckles, were growing less and less nimble. Once again, he attempted to apply a bit of pressure to the keyhole.

But this time, the tip of the pen broke against the lock and a splash of ink covered his fingertips. The ink was slippery between his fingers and it ran off of the bones of his wrist. He dropped the pen in the dirt once more and woefully wiped the ink from his hands onto the backpack. He was tired and leaned his weight into the trunk resting his head on his shoulder. Trying to think of a better plan, he drifted in and out of consciousness.

When Clay Morris awoke, he sat in the dirt looking up at the sky through the tree branches. The moon was offering a diminutive amount of light and a scattering of clouds was doing its best to hide what little sky there was. His teeth had been chattering for a while even while he slept but as he had drifted off and lost track of time, they too must have lost faith in what they were doing and given up their chatter hours ago. The midway point of the night was now long passed and the morning hours were drawing nearer.

It's now or never, I guess. Clay reached around for the bag and drew another pen from the large open pocket. This time, he tried breaking the small arm off from the side of the pen, the piece designed to clip the pen onto shirt pockets or clipboards. The new metal arm broke off so that it had a small hook on the end. He used the hook to pull on the edge of the keyhole opposite where a key's teeth would slide in, giving him ample room to insert the kilt pin that thankfully, had stayed gripped in his cramped, numb hand throughout the night. He fiddled with the kilt pin, applying constant pressure with the piece fashioned from the pen, until he felt a click. The core structure of the lock clinked as he must have forced one of the internal lock pins into the correct position. He gained confidence and tried again, sliding the kilt pin slightly out of the hole. Again it clinked. Once again he withdrew a bit more of the fine metal point.

Click.

The locked popped opened in his palm.

The chains were shaken to the ground and he wriggled free. Clay stood in the dawn's light arching his back and stretching. His ribs poked at his abdomen from the inside causing him to wince. Like a bloody zombie, Clay limped cautiously, slowly and stiff-legged, careful not to slip on the dew covered rocks and roots along the pathways. Clay couldn't help but think about what he was going to do as he started home initially down the trails along the creek and then the broader trails that snaked through the woods.

Should I tell someone what Jay did to her? As horrific as it had been for her, she didn't even bother trying to get me off of the tree. She just left. Clay struggled with weighing the options as he walked in the direction of his home.

I should tell the police. I have to. Maybe I should get her to tell the police and I can be there to help her when she does it? He reminded himself of the fact that he had never had the courage to tell anyone about the bullying he had been a victim of his entire life. It was his fault it escalated this much. He had never told the doctors or the police what had happened outside of 7-11. He had never told the teachers about the dragging down the hill at school or his parents about when Mark had picked him up to play football and dropped him off miles from home. Nor had he ever mentioned to anyone even the smallest detail of the incident with Myles after Halloween.

If only I would have said something sooner. A Change Is Gonna Come, he thought. Sunlight was starting to peak into the valley, yet the forest was doing its best to hold onto the night. *I'm not letting this guy kill me off.* Clay stopped and looked at his watch. It read 8:33am.

By far it had been the longest and worst night of his life. He changed directions on the path and started heading to Stonebridge Academy instead.

Chapter XXXVI-

That same morning, Jason and his friends were as ready as they could have been, having stayed up the better part of the night memorizing the work that Clay had written for them. They arrived at Pine Creek Community High School bright and early for their exams, confident that they would all be scoring very well on the English test in the morning, followed by mathematics in the afternoon. The following day, they would need to write either history or geography depending on which class they had enrolled in at the start of the year and then they'd have their biology exam. In the coming days after that, they would each have a couple other finals, including Leon's calculus one, which they would do their best on, knowing their overall averages would be climbing after strong performances on some of the key exams; thanks to a little strategic planning and Clay's help. Their plot was coming together beautifully.

Clay on the other hand, was somberly making his way through the woods. The daylight broke through the trees completely and began to energize him. He limped along the path. The dried mixture of pine and fir needles softened each step, while ribs struggled to pop back into place, dried blood hardened around his nose and lower lip and blue ink covered his hands. As he moved through the trees, he played with a loose tooth in his mouth pushing it back in place with his tongue. *Nobody is going to stop me from getting out of this town.*

Strangely, at Pine Creek Community High School, those students who seemed best prepared to cheat their way through a test, almost always were the best prepared with their supplies upon entering an exam room. Mark, Jason, Leon, William, Nathan and Billy walked into their school's gymnasium: a grand sized, but run down, wooden room.

They entered together, smiling and self-assured in stride. The gym was damp and musky, smelling of years' worth of sweat and few victories. The school logo of a cartoonish panther mascot was painted on the far wall with a motto beneath it proudly proclaiming, "One team in victory." Fittingly, last season, the school's basketball team had but one victory. The pathetic few white championship banners hanging from the rafters from better years now long gone had become stained yellow with age. Rows of individual tables and chairs stretched from wall to wall. It was in this gymnasium that all of the students would write each of their final exams every June.

When the boys entered the room, they drew the attention of a few of the teachers assigned to supervise the first exam of the week. Knowing their character, the teachers proceeded to separate the boys and asked them to sit in various corners of the room. The boys obligingly dispersed from one another and took their seats, content knowing they had all of Clay's correct responses committed to memory already.

As the last few students filtered into the gymnasium, Jay took a look around for Dallas. She was nowhere to be seen- *Perhaps he had been too rough on her,* he thought to himself. *Then again, she had it coming for hanging around that Tree Hugger.*

Emerging from the forest, Clay looked as if he had crossed a battlefield when he stumbled up to Stonebridge Academy, pushed his way through the large doors and limped into the building. He first headed to his locker, where he always kept a spare set of formal clothes. The school had a history of requiring students to wear formal uniforms for special days, final exam days included, and many of the students kept an extra set in their lockers just in case they forgot. It took him a couple of times before he managed to spin the correct combination on his locked locker, but once he gained access to the contents inside, he promptly grabbed the uniform items, slammed the door shut and hooked the lock back on the front.

Looking down at his disheveled self in his tattered street clothes with his hair matted and messed and his face red and dirty, he opted to head to the washroom to get changed and attempt to clean up. As he limped through the hallway, he stood out amongst the other teens zigzagging about in their freshly pressed uniforms. Yet, with everyone scurrying to their classrooms overwhelmed with last minute prepping for exams, not a single peer mentioned anything about his appearance.

Clay swung open the bathroom door, feeling his ribs pinch his insides in the process. He checked the stalls making sure the room was empty, then flipped the deadbolt across on the door to make sure there would be no unexpected intruders. Clay undressed and tossed the shreds of clothes he'd been wearing into the waste basket.

The clean formal uniform pieces gave him a feeling of self-transformation as he put them on. He didn't have his dress shoes with him, but nobody was likely going to notice. Looking into the mirror, he could see from the damage done to his face that the transformation was far from complete. He stepped up to the sink, turned the knob and began to splash the warm water flowing from the tap onto his face and neck. Red water riddled with dirt spiralled down the drain. The mirror showed his hair needed a bit of a rinse as well, so he leaned forward and washed it quickly in the sink, picking out the clumps of soil and dried blood with his fingertips.

Hopefully that does the trick, Clay thought as he grabbed some paper towels and used them to dry his face and hair. *I have to hurry to my exam.*

Disoriented, he headed to the school's gymnasium where he expected to write his exams. When he arrived, he discovered it was currently off limits to students as it was receiving its customary, yearly coat of fresh varnish. Though the gym floor at Stonebridge was used often, it never appeared worn; instead, it was polished to a high gloss.

Alone in the grand space, Clay stood there and shook his wrist. The motion snapped a few crimson drops of blood that had run secretively from his elbow beneath his blazer and down his sleeve, onto the polished gym surface. He gave his head a little shake back and forth trying to figure out where he was supposed to go to write the exams. It came to him in a moment of clarity. *Oh yeah.*

Exams would be taking place soon in classrooms throughout the school and he had to get to the physics lab. The school administration figured that students should write their exams in the locations where they had learned the majority of their course material. Clay Morris left the gym feeling secure that his appearance would pass until he actually got seated at a desk in the physics room.

The young girl sitting at the desk beside him noticed his rough appearance: dirty running shoes, red cheeks and wet collar from when he had washed his face and asked, "Are you alright?"

"Yeah, I'll be alright. Thanks." Clay politely responded instinctively even though his mind was wrought with other things. She sat there confused as to why he looked the way he did but didn't push for details. "Can I borrow a pencil?" he said.

The girl dug through her pencil case sitting neatly organized at the corner of her desk until she found one and handed it over.

"Thanks."

As she leaned toward him to offer the pencil, she caught a whiff of urine. Unsure what to think of the situation she straightened out in her chair and turned her focus instead to the test, which was already waiting face down on her desk. It has been put there beforehand by the instructor, who was now standing at the front of the room reminding everyone to read carefully, show their work and watch the time.

On the starting signal by the professor, the students all flipped their exams over in unison. Clay kept his head down as he turned his paper over; doing his best not to be noticed by anyone else.

"You may all begin," the teacher proclaimed, checking the clock on the wall. The tall figure at the front of the room took a moment to write the starting time of the exam in large font on a portable white board that had been rolled into the room. Clay watched her scribe the perfectly linear black numbers on the board with a dry erase marker. Again, he gently snapped his head, cocking his chin to the side realizing the trouble he was in. He had borrowed a pencil, but had not thought of a calculator and this physics exam was going to be difficult without one. Loathing his error, the young man scowled and pulled the edge of his upper lip into a sneer. *Gotta try*, he thought as he lifted his weighty pencil and began to read the instructions on page one.

Clay was partway through the exam before the teacher had made her way past his desk and noticed his running shoes. They were dirty, with pine needles sticking out from between the tongue and laces. She too saw the damp neckline of his shirt, but because his head was turned down towards his desk, she merely figured he must have been sweating from the stress of the exam.

"Are you OK, Clay?" she asked, quietly noticing the absence of a calculator.

Clay raised his head only slightly to see the face of the woman speaking to him. As he did so, she noticed the reams of scribbled calculations in smudged pencil lead on his test booklet. He responded, "Yes, but can I talk to you after the exam? I just want to write it first."

She noticed his face looked as though he had been through some struggle and there appeared to be a touch of blood around his nose. Concerned, but also completely confused, and understanding his desire to finish undisturbed, she decided to let him continue while she kept her eye on him.

"That's fine, but please come and speak to me or Mr. Isaacs when you hand it in. He'll be popping in during the exam," she whispered.

His teacher then continued down the aisle of desks and walked back up to the front of the classroom near her desk. He went back to his calculating. Clay was just getting back into a difficult question when she returned moments later and slid an extra, small, simple functioning calculator on his desk next to his exam booklet. He looked up at her once more catching her smiling at him.

"And I'll let the shoes slide this once," she whispered. "Just give it back when you are finished, please. It's my spare."

He nodded in agreement and turned his gaze to the stack of stapled white pages smeared with answers in front of him. She smiled and slipped away in silence.

Clay ripped through the remainder of the exam. He took time every now and then, when the questions were a little more difficult, to sit up straight and breathe a few times deeply while contemplating solutions. They always seemed to come to him in due time. Compared to the practice work he had been doing throughout the semester, this material was easy for him even though the questions were nothing like he had expected.

The use of a calculator allowed him to skip a lot of writing and Clay found he had plenty of time to go back and check his earlier work, which had all been done by calculating everything by hand. He was quite amused with himself when he discovered that one by one, without exception, each of his initial responses involving significant number crunching had been verified by the calculator.

Across town, Jason and the others sat at their desks in the Pine Creek gymnasium where the painted lines on the floor indicating various courts were chipped and peeling. The papers were handed out one by one by several of the adults in the room. The students were instructed to leave them face down until told to turn them over. Once all had been handed out, the signal was given and uneager students across the gym timidly flipped the sheets and began writing.

Jason turned his over and read the top of the page: Pine Creek Community High School- English 12 Final Exam. He smiled for an instant before he noticed the year in the top corner of the front page. It was last year's date. He suddenly noticed how hot and stuffy the room had become. Looking over at Mark, it seemed he too had noticed.

Mark shrugged his shoulders and then saw a teacher with her eyes directed at him, so he turned back toward his exam and began writing.

For a second, Jason Blithe sensed something was off. Worried, he read the first question and recognized it as one he had memorized from Clay's notes. He chalked the date mistake up as a type-o and continued writing the answers in order as he had memorized them during the night for each number on the test, not bothering to waste any more time reading a single other question as he went.

Chapter XXXVII-

Clay finished checking over the last question of the day's exam. He paused for a moment before getting up from the desk. *I have* to, he thought. Clay carried his paper to the front of the room where the physics teacher was waiting at a table talking to the principal of Stonebridge Academy, Mr. Arthur Isaacs, who sat in the chair next to her. He placed the calculator down on the table in front of his teacher.

"Thanks again for that." Then Clay dropped his test next to it onto the stack of papers that had been handed in before his and said with a quiver in his voice, "Can we talk please sir?"

He was able to look Mr. Isaacs in the eyes only for a moment, for when the principal rose from his seat to address him, he was much taller than the teenage boy. Clay found himself looking up at the underside of the principal's immense square jaw.

Mr. Isaacs had been tipped off by the other teacher that Clay looked quite disheveled and may need to talk and so he agreed and walked Clay out of the classroom to his office. As they stepped through the doorway leaving the physics classroom, Mr. Isaacs moved aside to let his student pass first. The giant of a man looked closely at Clay and wondered what could have happened to the boy's face to cause such bruising. Mr. Isaac's low voice bellowed as he requested the student make his way down a series of hallways to his office.

As Clay walked single-file in front of Mr. Isaacs, he recalled the last time he had been asked to go to the principal's office- It was the substitute that had pissed him off at Pine Creek. *Please let things go better this time*, he hoped.

In the privacy of Mr. Isaacs' office, with the door sealed tightly and the window shades drawn, Clay felt sheltered and protected. It was somewhat calming and he sat down bravely in the warm cloth chair opposite his principal who looked like a mountain stationed behind his grand cherry stained wooden desk. Fearful that he might change his mind about being willing to talk, Clay started unloading things off of his chest faster than he could think. Only at this point, he remained cautious about what information he was providing. He was torn between telling someone what had been happening to him for so long and keeping the secrets burning within him for fear that now others would be hurt if he told.

Mr. Isaacs scanned the young man trying to decipher why he was such a mess physically while Clay carried on telling Mr. Isaacs about what had happened to him the night before, starting with how he had been beaten up in the forest by Jason and his friends.

"Are you alright? I mean, physically? Are you all right?" the man repeated. He could see the pain on the boy's face as he answered.

"I think so, but I'm not sure." Clay was squeamish responding to the question and he wormed back and forth in his seat refusing to make eye contact. The physical injuries were more than telling and the principal could see Clay was hurting by his timid demeanor and his half-closed saddened eyes, which peered at the patchwork shades of brown squares forming an artistically modern pattern on the carpet.

Clay wasn't sure how much more to say. He didn't want to go too far and tell the man everything; just enough that there may be a little justice handed down. It didn't matter because the man cut him off before he could continue any further.

"I'm going to ask that you see Ms Gustavson to make sure you're alright. Can you do that young man?"

Ms Gustavson was the school nurse. Clay didn't really want to speak to her, and he sure as hell wasn't going to be physically examined by her, but he conceded realizing it wasn't really an option he was provided.

Mr. Isaacs had heard about occasional rumors of fighting between the two schools in the past so he didn't seem overly concerned with the bullying at first. And given that Clay had only attended his school for a year, he hadn't really had much time to get to know Clay well enough personally to know whether he was partly to blame for whatever had taken place. But, as principal of a prestigious school, he did not want his student's involved in any shady behaviour whatsoever. The next words out of his stern mouth were terrifying for Clay.

Mr. Isaacs was not one to jump to conclusions and he figured it would be best to hold a meeting with the other student and the principal from Pine Creek Community High School. It would be the easiest way to get to the bottom of things. Arthur Isaacs asked Clay to move into the boardroom adjoining his office, while he picked up the phone and made a direct call to the other school.

Clay began to second guess himself for speaking about the ordeal. He got up from his chair and walked into the neighboring room awaiting Mr. Isaacs' phone conversation with the principal of his old school. He sat down in one of the chairs around the table and listened intently. Clay could hear the discussion that was taking place and knew shortly, that Jason would end up right there with him, sitting across the table. He shuddered at the thought. Clay heard the phone click as it was being hung up. Mr Isaacs thumped his way into the boardroom.

"They'll be a while getting here, Clay. Why don't I send you over to see Ms Gustavson and she can have a look at you?" Mr. Isaacs eyed Clay's face once more, noting the variety of colors from his multitude of bruises and bumps.

"OK." Clay rose from his seat and left the boardroom. Clay had heard from peers that Ms Gustavson was a kind, middle aged woman, and the school's nurse. She was soft spoken, well-liked by the student body and always smelled of strong, but expensive, perfume. By the time he made it to within a few feet of her office, he could already smell the scent of her perfume. He walked in to find that she had been expecting him; both his physics teacher and Mr. Isaacs had made phone calls.

Ms Gustavson spent a great deal of time assessing Clay for injuries. He sat motionless and speechless on her examination table. Though she smelled pretty, her appearance seemed a little old and haggard. She had oily skin and hair that looked like it had been in rollers at one time. And her hair was far too long for someone her age. But she was indeed soft spoken and kind. Her hands were soft to touch and her veins were quite evident through her thin skin. Under the fragrance of expensive perfume, she smelled like old people; an odor Clay remembered from visits to his grandparents' house on the coast.

"Got yourself into some trouble, did you son?"

Clay was in no mood to discuss the matter.

She took his silence as a request for her to hurry up and get the job done. She cleaned him up and applied some gauze to various areas, securing each patch with a few strips of surgical tape and then handed him an ice pack and told him to relax for a while. "I'll come and get you when it's time to go see Mr. Isaacs again. I'm going to phone your mother."

Realizing that his mother has still not heard about his whereabouts and was probably worried sick, he thanked her. "Thanks. Just tell her I'm alright." Clay lay down on the table and held the ice pack to his cheekbone. It stung a little but his ribs were more bothersome and he concentrated on breathing slowly and shallowly so that they wouldn't cause too much discomfort.

Clay must have drifted off to sleep for a while, for when Ms Gustavson woke him, the ice pack was thawed on the ground beside the examination table. She calmly asked that he head back to the board room for his meeting with Mr. Isaacs. Clay agreed, knowing it would just be the two of them there.

When he arrived back in the boardroom, nobody was present, so he took his seat once again at the grand meeting table. *I guess they weren't quite ready for me yet,* he thought. He could hear Mr. Isaacs typing on a keyboard in his office next door. It was a fairly long, excruciating wait for Clay in the boardroom. He had finally decided he wanted to tell someone about just one of his ordeals and he was being put on hold. It was painful, but he was determined to wait until he'd get his chance to confront the bully who had taken so much from him through the years.

Mr. Isaacs did not wait in the room with him; he stayed in his office working at his computer. *Sometimes delayed gratification seemed like punishment*, Clay thought as he could feel butterflies in his stomach churning as if they were personally making ulcers.

Suddenly, Mr. Isaacs' secretary showed up with the principal from Pine Creek and Jason in tow. She asked them to take a seat at the table in the boardroom while she fetched her boss who had already taken note that they had arrived and was beginning to make his way into the room from the door of his office. Jason's eyes, which seemed at first to be admiring the splendor of the boardroom, shifted and fixed on Clay's.

"What seems to be the problem, Art?" The other principal asked.

"I'll let the story come from the boy's mouth," said Mr. Isaacs.

Clay did not like his choice of the word "story." Again, Clay skipped everything but the last few hours of the night when he explained what had happened and how Jason had been the ringleader of the assault. Jason, who couldn't help but notice the gauze taped on Clay's face, sat there stabbing Clay with his eyes and grinding his teeth loudly as Clay persisted with describing the part where he was tied to the tree and urinated on. The others in the room were a bit taken aback at the brutality of it. Even Mr. Isaacs squirmed in his chair as Clay had neglected to include those pieces of information in his first telling. There was still no mention of the kidnapping, gun, cheating, or rape.

The principals then turned to Jason and asked for his side of the story. He instantly took his chance to deny the severity of the events and then went on to tell the adults a lie about how he had only beaten him up because Clay had spitefully stolen his girlfriend. Jason had kept his version short and to the point, purposefully not giving many details to avoid being caught up in his lie should someone question him further.

"He's lying!" Clay shouted.

"Clay. Quiet down please," said Mr. Isaacs attempting to keep a hold of the situation.

"Whatever," Jason said slouching in his chair.

"He beat me up… And he's a cheater," Clay divulged more than he had intended. His chest was pounding only to be muffled by his rapid and deep breathing.

"What?" Jason tried his best to sound surprised.

"He's a cheater." Clay paused for a moment to catch his breath. "He and his friends stole the exams and made me do the questions while they threatened me!" Clay knew that the cat was now out of the bag. He might as well tell them everything from last night.

"You're the cheater. You asked us to steal some tests from your school." Jason fought back. "But we wouldn't. My friends and I aren't like that."

"That's a lie! And I can prove it!" Clay could hold back no further but didn't know what to say to make them believe his story more than Jason's. He knew he had written the answers to the biology test. He also knew that the only way his attackers could have gotten those tests was to take them from the offices of the teachers. One of those offices used to belong to Mr. Kent.

Clay was grasping at straws but he thought there might be a chance that Kent's video camera outside his office in the Annex could have caught them on film stealing the tests. He began to explain the whereabouts of the camera and how Mr. Kent had set it up to loop through the tape and reset each day. "They'll be on tape. They'll have to be on tape."

Both adults in the room sat there dumfounded about what was being told to them. The story seemed too elaborate to be possible but had enough elements of truth buried within that it couldn't be completely brushed aside as a kid just having some kind of mental breakdown during the toughest part of the year academically.

"Your fucking dead," Jason spoke much too calmly given his company in the room and his eyes glazed over as if nothing lay behind them.

"These are some serious allegations, young man." The Pine Creek employee commented while looking sternly at Jason sitting there steaming.

Mr. Isaacs, already a fairly large and imposing man, sat up in his chair and leaned closer. The display was enough that Clay knew Isaacs was backing his student.

The principal from Pine Creek continued, "But, then again… we've also had some other questions arise about Jason's character this morning."

"Oh?" said Mr. Isaacs subtly suggesting more be told.

"I'll tell you what. It's getting late today and there's a lot of stuff we are going to have to check in on tomorrow to make sure we get the facts straight. It sounds like these boys are pretty worked up. Why don't we send these boys home for the night and we can call them back in for another meeting in the morning with their parents? We can have one of the auxiliary police officers sit in on it if need be."

These auxiliary officers were part-time members of the police force. They were paid employees who took active roles in the school communities dealing with any offenses that were deemed illegal and requiring a police presence or investigation.

"That sounds fine," Mr. Isaacs agreed.

Clay could barely believe what he was hearing. "I just told you this kid cheated on the finals and beat the shit out of me and you aren't going to do anything about it right now because it's getting late?"

"That's enough for now son. I'll call Mrs. Blithe to come get Jason from Pine Creek School. I'll walk him back there and hand him over to his mom." The Pine Creek principal stood up from the table and pushed his chair in. "Jason, you are going to have to go straight home with your folks, alright?"

Jason couldn't believe what he was hearing either. They were going to send him home. He was going to get away with this.

"Alright?" the principal repeated.

"OK." Jason knew he was getting off easy and had some things he desperately needed to take care of.

Jason sneered at Clay with a look so evil it reached across the table at him and Clay knew within moments his enemy would be heading straight back to his school to look for the camera. With that, Jason was ushered out the door by his administrator who followed right behind.

Mr. Isaacs brought Clay to the front entrance of the school and saw to it that Jason and the other administrator were past the fountain and long gone on their way back to Pine Creek before seeing him off. "We'll see you tomorrow, Clay. Better get your story straight. I'm worried that you're caught up in something serious here, son," he said.

Chapter XXXVIII-

It was now closing in on the late afternoon and Clay's stomach was aching. He realized he hadn't eaten since breakfast the day before. *Maybe some of it didn't happen. Maybe I just made some of it up? I haven't slept and Jason and these tests are stressing me out. Could it have been that bad? Why did no one else believe me?* Clay was seriously beginning to question his own sanity. He was just stepping away from the front doors wandering towards the fountain deep in thought when Dallas showed up from around the corner of the building.

"Hey," she said.

"Hey," Clay replied happy to see her. "You OK?"

"Not really." Dallas began to tear up. She struggled to not let herself blink as it would cause the tears welling up in her eyes to stream down her cheeks. "How about you?"

"I don't know either." Clay was somber in his tone and he walked over to the school's fountain and sat down on the marble edge of the pool; the water splashing behind him.

Dallas came and sat down beside him. She reached over and took his hand gently in hers.

"Really, are you OK?" Clay pressed her to see if she would give him any indication that she was alright.

"We've got to do something," Dallas said, doing her best to change the subject in order to avoid the pain that thinking about the previous night's events would cause. Unable to hold back any longer, she blinked a few times causing tears to cascade down her face. Her mascara had already smudged enough to make her face appear dark and hollow. Dallas turned toward Clay squeezing his hand tighter in her fingers.

Clay looked at her closely and could see her eyes gradually changing from sadness to anger. Her voice became sterner as she told Clay how she had gone into school early to talk to the guidance counselor.

"I told Ms Thompson that I heard somebody may have stolen the finals. I guess they were worried after noticing some broken ceiling tiles or something? She spread the word to the rest of the staff and I think they were doing some last minute planning to use an alternate test for each of their classes just in case." She really hadn't known how any cheating had taken place; just what snippets she had overheard in the forest, but Clay really hoped what she had said about the teachers switching the tests was true. She continued to fill Clay in on how she had been excused from the day's tests.

"I told them about how they all cheated and beat me up," he said.

"You did?" Dallas stood there with her eyebrows raised and her lower jaw hanging. The surprised look on her face remained while she added, "What did they say?"

Clay explained how he had told Mr. Isaacs about their cheating plan and how he had been forced to do the exams for them last night before arriving at the forest.

Dallas had already noticed that even though he had changed clothes and had been patched up, he was still badly bruised and scratched and quite dirty from the night before. She nodded with approval.

"I don't think they even believed me. Jason told them some big lie about how I stole his girlfriend."

Dallas gave the slight hint of a smile. It was just big enough that Clay noticed. "Did...did you say anything to Ms Thompson about what happened to you last night?"

"What do you mean?" Dallas pretended not to know.

"You know. About what happened in the forest?" Clay knew he was treading on hollow ground by asking the question.

"I couldn't. I doubt they'd believe me either. I'm just some screwed up girl with a history of being depressed and the school slut."

Clay could see by her face she was hurting while saying the last few words.

"Besides, he has all his buddies to back up his side of the story."

"We could take him down," Clay said, half asking and half suggesting. He went on to tell her about the possibility of Kent's camera having the group stealing the tests on tape and how Jason was likely on his way to the school to find it. "We'd have to stop him from getting the video though."

"I'm in. We need to make that asshole pay for what he did."
Dallas had all the motivation she needed and now, with even just one
person on her side, she felt ready to take on the world.

"What's the plan?" Clay asked.

Before he could even get the words out, Dallas had sprung
into action. She was off and running making her way to the pathway
twisting into trees that made up the expansive forest dividing the two
schools. Clay ran off after her not sure of what her plan was. She
was quick, jumping over roots and ducking from low hanging
spruce, fir and pine branches and Clay had to run as fast as he could
manage considering how badly his body hurt just to keep sight of her
as she darted down the trails. The forest floor felt hard and dry
below his feet, twigs crackled as he stepped on them with his long
lanky strides and the sounds only reminded him further of the
intensity of his broken ribs. Pulling up lame for a moment, Clay
held his side, coughed, and spat a glob of blood into the bushes
nearby. Dallas's hair seemed to fly behind her like a cape as she
sped away and finally out of sight.

When Clay finally caught his breath and the flare up of pain
had toned down enough for him to proceed with his chase, he
continued on down the main link of pathways. He arrived at the
school, instinctively exited the forest and headed around the central
building towards the smaller Annex. There she was: standing
peering around the corner of the building. She had pulled out her
smart phone and was videotaping Jason from a distance as he was
entering the Annex building. Clay came up beside her.

"How's this for proof?" she said. He could see Jason in the distance. "But, we're gonna need more than this to be sure people believe us." Dallas reached into the top of her low hanging shirt and stuffed her phone into the cleavage of her chest before jolting towards the Annex entrance, whipping open the doors and disappearing inside.

Clay took after her, again, trying to catch his breath. He grabbed the door handle and realized it was unlocked. *Must have been left unlocked by the teachers*, he thought. In fact, the janitor had been working again and had unlocked the doors during her shift as usual, none the wiser that her daily work habits had been part of an extensive break and entry plot the night before. Clay could hear Dallas heading up the stairwell so he followed cautiously and with hopes that Jason would not be around to spot them. As he reached the landing on the top floor, Dallas stood there watching through the glass doors.

"Do you see him?" Clay asked.

Dallas stood there in silence. She turned to face him holding her right index finger up to her mouth to quiet her friend. "He's down the hall looking up at the roof," Dallas whispered back.

Clay nodded showing he understood the need to remain undetected and positioned himself so that he too could see through the doors. Their shoulders touched as they watched and tried to determine what to do next.

Dallas could smell Clay's shirt. He stunk of urine and sweat, but she said nothing as she held her spot next to him. *This guy has been through as much as I have and we're in this together*, she thought.

"Keep taping him," Clay suggested. Dallas took her phone out from her chest and with a couple of swipes began filming through the glass. She zoomed in trying to get a clearer image. The two of them stood in silence as they watched what was taking place through the small screen on her phone; Jason's figure digitally magnified in front of them on the tiny hand-held device. They maintained their video surveillance as Jay appeared to be searching the ceiling for something.

"Must be looking for Mr. Kent's video camera. He's right by it."

Dallas zoomed in further and tapped the screen over the image of Jason to bring it into focus. The figure down the hall climbed atop the lockers and reached up to a metallic, smoke alarm-looking appliance attached to the roof. Jason fumbled with the device trying to figure out how it was attached to the roof. It didn't take long before he pulled off the metal housing over the video recorder and set it down by his feet on the lockers. Inside, he had revealed what was, only a few years ago, a state of the art video recorder. Then, with the push of a button, he ejected a small black tape.

Both Dallas and Clay stared intently at the screen which illuminated close up what was happening in real time only a few dozen yards away. Jason took the tape in his hand and climbed down from the lockers leaving the video machine hanging wide open above. As he stared at the device in his palm, he pulled back the small piece of plastic guarding the tape itself and with his free hand, started pulling the spool of tape out. The dark brown ribbons of film footage piled on the floor as he pulled strand after strand. Once all the film had been stripped from the tape's spools, he gathered the pile from the floor into a crumpled bundle and tossed it into the nearby silver colored, metal trashcan.

Nobody can find out. I've gotta get rid of this tape, he thought, desperately thinking of a way to completely destroy the evidence.

The spies could just make out what he was doing as he extracted a lighter from his back pocket, crouched down next to the garbage can and lit the crumpled mess in the bin. No flames were visible on Dallas's camera phone, but they could tell by the small plumes of smoke billowing from the trashcan that he had ignited the only other proof aside from what she held in her hand that could have corroborated their story about Jay's cheating.

Jason didn't stay to watch it burn. Once he was confident it was smoldering away in the trash, he turned and started walking back towards them down the hallway. Once more, his walked turned into a swagger as he drew nearer the two hiding behind the door. Jason's image grew in size on the phone's screen.

"He's coming! We need to go. Now!" Clay grabbed Dallas by the arm and tugged her away from the door. They ran down the stairs attempting to stay as quiet as possible by running on the balls of their feet as if they were actually tip toeing. When they reached the main floor landing, Dallas tried to push open the doors to go back outside, but Clay, still holding her wrist, pulled her back in.

"He'll see us. We need to hide." He turned and kicked open the doors leading into the main floor of the Annex. The two of them entered the hallway and then ducked into the hollowed out space of a doorway leading into one of the workshop classrooms.

They stood silently listening first to the sounds of the upper doorway swinging open then followed by footsteps down the stairs. Clay couldn't help but to peak from the doorway. He could see Jason stopping for a moment and looking back up the stairs from whence he had just come before exiting the Annex doors, out onto the school grounds, and heading off home.

"I want to see it," said Dallas.

Clay who was still watching the outer doors turned to her. His eyes agreed and the two of them went back upstairs. When they arrived at Mr. Kent's office, Clay stopped for a moment and glanced up at the video camera still mounted to the roof, free of its housing. *What if Mr. Kent had never put this here?* He was starting to imagine how his life would have been different when Dallas interjected and called him over to where the coils of film sat smoldering in the metal trash can. The original evidence was gone; a melted combination of flaming and charred tape- all that remained was the video footage Dallas had just taken on her phone.

"I thought of a way we could get even with him forever." Dallas looked at Clay with a glimmer in her hazel eyes. This sparkle was something Clay hadn't seen since the moment when she had given him her kilt pin and he knew she was up to something. He looked over at her staring intently at the last flickering strips of film in the garbage. Dallas brushed away her bangs and grabbed the trashcan.

"I'm in," he echoed the comment she had made earlier; knowing the two of them would be linked to this instance forever.

Chapter XXXIX-

The sun made the mistake of rising early today. It seemed to climb into the sky sooner than normal and with the eagerness and hue that suggested it should be the beginning of a bright new day. It has made a mistake though. This was not the start of any particular day someone would want to remember; except for Clay. He had waited a long time for this day.

Dallas had spent the night at his place. Clay's mother, happy to finally have Clay home, could sense when they walked into the house that the two of them had had a rough night. Clay, covered in bandages, looked as though he had been beaten up again and his ex-girlfriend looked as if she was the only one around to console him. Mrs. Morris allowed Dallas to stay on the couch in the living room for the night, provided, when she called home to ask, it was alright with her parents- and of course it was.

When Clay awoke that morning, he came downstairs to find his mother having breakfast with Dallas at the kitchen table. She had been talking to Dallas about what she had overheard on the local radio when the alarm had awakened her. It was something about a fire. It seemed someone had set fire to the Annex building of Pine Creek Community High School and overnight the entire school had burned uncontrollably to the ground. There was nothing the fire department could do to stop the blaze.

Clay sat down next to Dallas and placed his hand on hers as he pulled his chair closer to the table. He gave her a smile before helping himself to a bowl of cereal.

"Clay, your principal, Mr. Isaacs, also called last night. I guess we have some meeting with him this morning and apparently a police officer will be there. Do you know anything about this?" Mrs. Morris asked. "You sure have some explaining to do to me about where you ended up last night. I was sure something terrible had happened."

If only she knew, Clay thought, looking again over to Dallas. "Don't worry mom, everything is fine. I just got beat up again. It was Ms Gustavson at Stonebridge who patched me up so Mr. Isaacs probably just wants you to be informed." Clay turned to Dallas and gave her a knowing smirk.

Chapter XL-

After breakfast, Clay got up from the table realizing this was the day when things would finally change for him. Mrs. Morris and Dallas were already putting on their shoes at the front door. For once, Dallas' body looked frail and weak, though she smiled at him as he caught a glimpse of her stuffing her phone into her front pocket, and the way she ushered him to come along quickly indicated that there was more life in this girl yet.

The three of them piled into Mrs. Morris' old sedan and she drove them to Stonebridge Academy where they were met at the front door by Mr. Isaacs who led them to the boardroom table in the meeting room near his office. Already sitting at the far end of the table were the principal from Pine Creek Community High School, Jason Blithe and his disgruntled parents, neither of whom looked very impressed by the unfamiliar and unwanted situation they were in.

A female auxiliary officer had also shown up and had been seated along with one of her full-time police counterparts who sat with a black leather notepad laid out in front of him. She was in her mid-forties, with more grey hair than not. He seemed slightly older, yet had only hints of grey in his pronounced beard. Some scribbled records had already been written on his pad and he seemed eager to get the meeting started.

Mr. Isaacs shook the hands of both officers and thanked them again for coming, then pulled a chair out just far enough so that his potbelly pushed against the edge of the table as he sat next to them.

Jason glanced at Dallas for a moment. *What the hell is she doing here?*

Dallas, looking up at Mr. and Mrs. Blithe, could see that Jason had his father's stature but his mother's eyes; full of anger and resentment.

Then the suspect turned his head to lock his gaze on Clay's, warning him to keep his mouth shut. Clay was having none of it today and he would not back down, boldly staring right back at him. Clay pulled out a chair for his mother and one for Dallas too, before taking the final remaining seat at the table.

Assembled around the table, seated in their high back, brown leather chairs, was an audience there to bear witness to Jason's demise.

Mr. Isaacs opened the meeting by introducing Clay and Mrs. Morris to the officers and to Jason's parents. Clay took a second to introduce Dallas and explain she was there for support and that she could help explain some things. Mrs. Morris politely said her hellos and shook hands with the police officers across the tabletop. When she attempted to do the same to Mrs. Blithe, the offering of her outstretched hand was neglected and she retracted it. Feeling the unfriendliness in the room, Mrs. Morris sat back into her chair and crossed her arms across the table. Clay put his hand on her forearm in an attempt to console her as she tried to figure out what was going on.

"Now we've already heard from Jason this morning and you'd made some pretty serious accusations yesterday, Clay. So, perhaps you can share your thoughts now that the police have agreed to be with us?" Mr. Isaacs was eager to get things sorted out as quickly as possible as it was obvious he was already busy enough with exam week and the added stress of this situation forcing its way to the front of his priority list was growing too much to handle in late June.

"Yes please, indeed," requested the other principal.

Jason must have been here early to try and get his story out before we arrived, Clay thought to himself. The young man was not swayed though. He turned to Dallas who gave him a slight nod and then he came out with it. He explained everything that had happened to him to the officers, including: the kidnapping from the library, the accusations of cheating, the threats with the gun, the confinement in Jason's basement, the beatings by all of the boys involved and the events in the forest. Purposefully, he left out the rape as it was Dallas' secret to share if she ever wanted to.

The room remained silent through the entirety of his proclamation; everyone unsure how much of it could possibly be real. The bearded officer had been busily scribing notes in his leather pad as Clay spoke. Mrs. Morris was visibly shaken hearing the brutality that her son had endured. Her cheeks flushed and tears pooled deeply in her eyes. Throughout the story, Mr. Blithe's jaw muscles clenched like a pit bull's and he was grinding his teeth loud enough that everyone in the room could hear the grating. Jason's eyes never left Clay's.

Clay finished, "We have proof that Jason burned down Pine Creek Community High School last night."

Several others in the room piped up at the same time with the breaking news and the suggestion of a way to validate the story.

"What?" Jason gasped.

"What?" said Mr. Isaacs as he struggled to perk his overweight body upright in his chair.

"Son?" said the male officer, his bearded mouth dropping open. The others sat stunned while the officer continued, "Go ahead young man."

"I think you need to take a look at something we caught on film last night." Clay was now speaking with an unfamiliar confidence; his eyes, full of vengeance, locked again on Jason's across the expanse of the table as he spoke. It was now Jason who was sweating. Dallas pulled the phone from her pocket, tapped and swiped it a couple of times and slid it across the table to the officer.

The cop held the screen up close to his face and tapped the screen one more time. He watched for a moment before angling it slightly towards his partner who adjusted her glasses and leaned in to watch the small screen. Flickering on the display was clear footage of Jason Blithe breaking into the school.

"The time when we took this is indicated in the top corner of the screen, Sir," Clay added.

"This is only minutes before the fire department was dispatched to the fire early yesterday evening," the auxiliary police officer said. She wriggled her nose under the frame of her glasses and watched as her partner again jotted some notes on his paper.

"This certainly is some interesting information, son. How did you come across it?" The man looked up from his pad. All eyes were now fixed on Clay.

"Who took the video?" the principal from Pine Creek School demanded.

"Who took the video?" repeated the male officer.

"I did," said Dallas. Clay grasped her hand under the table and then he interrupted.

"After I left the meeting here yesterday afternoon, I ran into Dallas. We knew Jason would head back to the other school to get that video I told Mr. Isaacs and the Pine Creek principal about. You know, the one showing him stealing tests. You two didn't believe me."

He turned toward Mr. Isaacs who was sitting stunned in his chair. "So," Clay took a deep breath in and continued, "we followed Jason to the school and taped him as he broke in. We also have a clip of him grabbing Mr. Kent's old video camera I'd told you about and lighting the fire in the Annex building. It should be the next one on the phone."

The officer, frowning, tapped the phone one last time and watched as the event played out in front of him.

"Hmmm. We are going to have to keep this phone for a while. Is that alright Miss?"

Dallas nodded in agreement.

"What were you doing in the area, miss?" The cop pressed for more information from her.

"I was there to see if Clay was OK. He was pretty badly beaten up. I…"

The cop scowled and interrupted, "How did you know he was hurt?"

"I was there with him in the forest the night before when Jason and his friends beat him up." Clay squeezed Dallas' hand tighter as she continued.

"He didn't say anything about you being there," the cop said, assuming she was now catching the girl in a lie.

"I was there!" She insisted. I saw it all. Jason had a gun… And he… He and his friends ganged up on Clay and they chained him to a tree!"

Mr. Isaacs could wait no further and cut her off again. "Clay, you never mentioned her last night."

"Umm," Clay was unsure where to go from here but Dallas continued her account of the night.

"I was raped," she said. This time she squeezed his hand under the table. "Jason raped me while Clay was tied to the tree. I ran home after because I was so terrified, but then came back to the forest the next morning to find Clay. He was already gone. I ended up going to my school and talking to the guidance counselor. You can check with Ms Thompson. I told her about the stolen tests and then I came here, to Stonebridge, hoping I would be able to find him."

"Oh dear," Mrs. Morris said softly. A lump had quickly formed in her throat.

The Blithes both scowled at their son in disbelief.

The officer spoke directly to Mr. Isaacs. "This is now a police matter and we will take it from here." Jason tried to get up from the table, but the male officer twisted in his chair, reached up with his broad hand and grabbed Jason by the shoulder, promptly sitting him back in his seat.

The man used one hand to continue holding the accused against the back of his seat, then raised up, and used to other to stuff the note pad into his back pocket before unclipping a set of shiny handcuffs from his belt and handing them to the female officer who was already pulling Jason's own hands behind his back. She held them in place and locked in one of his wrists, then snapped the cuffs against the other so that the hard steal swung around locking on the opposite side.

Jason's parents sat beside him dumbfounded and speechless as they watched the officers forcefully stand him up and walk him towards the frame of the door. Mrs. Blithe managed to mutter, "You are not my son. This can't be happening," as she slid into a state of complete denial.

The police woman paused long enough to look at Dallas and Clay and say, "The two of you will eventually have to come in for questioning, but I trust Mr. Isaacs and your parents will see to it that, if you need it, you'll get some medical attention first. We will be in touch with your families in the next few hours. You are free to head home if you like." Mrs. Blithe began to break down in tears, her sobs muffling out Mr. Blithe's cursing as the two followed the officers and their son out of the school to a car waiting in idle outside.

"I'm sorry," Mr. Isaacs said looking over at the pair of teens. "I think you'll both need a doctor to have a look at you. Can we call your mother, Dallas?"

She nodded. Clay turned to give her a hug. Mrs. Morris stood up from her chair and wrapped her arms around both of them.

Chapter XLI-

The days that followed saw Jason's life turn on itself. The video footage had been enough to convince the police to search the confinements of his basement suite under his parents' home. They quickly obtained a warrant to search the premises; however, Jason, refusing to cooperate and open his lock, forced them to break down his door to gain access.

Once inside, they found evidence of the tests that were stolen such as Clay's handwritten notes for the group. As well as the loaded hand gun issued to his father, they found enough marijuana to charge Jay with possession with intent to sell. Furthermore, Jason's computer was confiscated and thoroughly examined. In his email inbox they found the pictures that he had taken of Dallas in the forest after he had raped her.

Jason Blithe did get his chance to escape Pine Creek and Pine Creek Community High School. He was eventually sent upstate to a youth detention center to await trial. It seemed there was enough evidence to lock him up for a long time. Even his friends, who had all come under fire and been charged for various crimes by the police, were quick to offer to testify against Jason in exchange for lighter sentences of their own. None of the other boys would receive immunity and each would ultimately bring shame to his own family as justice was served one by one.

In the end, to salt their wounds, they all got busted cheating on the exams. Jason, Mark, Leon and the rest of their buddies had the same answers, which were those Clay had written for them and they had each memorized that night. The teachers, who had been tipped off from Dallas' meeting with Ms Thompson, were worried about the validity and security of their exams, so they had managed to print off and distribute new ones; copies of last year's exams to be precise. Aside from the first couple of questions, the exams were completely different from the ones that had been memorized. So, as a result, the hooligans had the wrong answers for everything- the same wrong answers.

Clay was given special permission to write his remaining exams a week or so later, once he felt he was ready. He took a few days to get his head straight and then contacted Mr. Isaacs to let him know that he was well prepared. Mr. Isaacs was kind enough to open the school on the weekend just for Clay and the young man banged through his remaining finals with ease. When the government results finally came in, Clay had demonstrated First Class Honors results in all courses. Mrs. Morris was very supportive of both Clay and Dallas as they mended physically and emotionally in the coming weeks.

Dallas had no permanent physical damage from her ordeal in the woods; though she did spend a number of afternoons with Mrs. Morris and Ms Thompson restoring her self-worth and healing her spirit. Clay, as requested, was with her every step of the way.

Chapter XLII-

High Street, a main corridor in Oxford, UK takes one past several of the colleges connected to the university before it comes to intersect with Cornmarket Street in front of an old clock tower. Clay stood at the base of the tower waiting for his meeting. His hair had grown a little over the summer and it was long enough that he needed to tuck it behind his ear.

He compared his watch to the large, historical timepiece in front of him. The clock, Carfax Tower as it is known, showed 3:35pm- the time when classes would finish back in Pine Creek each day of his childhood schooling. It was also the time when Clay knew he had made it through another day of anguish at the hands of his tormentors, even if by the narrowest of margins; though sometimes he would find out that making his way home was an equivalent part of the battle. As he stood looking up at the clock, watching the large minute hand move in its slow, sweeping arc, people seemed to pass by him in the street, busily scurrying off to university classes with books in hand. It was so very different from the schools in Pine Creek.

Clay had made his escape. His marks had been high enough across the board to secure his full scholarship to Oxford University and he was now joining these students in the start of the fall term. A flourishing relationship with Dallas would bring her out to visit within a couple of weeks and he was desperate to see her again.

A light rain began to fall while he stood there on the corner. The fires in his heart were washed out with each drop as they tapped on his face and shoulders. He smiled. This time, it was a real smile. One he could not hold back and one that stretched wide in the warm summer rain.

"Clay?" The unmistakeable voice of Mister Kent gave him away. Clay turned to see his mentor pushing a bicycle across the street with a book bag slung over his shoulder.

"Mr. Kent, there you are."

"Sorry I'm a tad late, but I'm glad you finally made it. I'll help you get settled now that you are in your first days of classes. And we'll see if we can get your new flat ready for Dallas when she arrives. Have I got some books for you..."

Made in the USA
San Bernardino, CA
28 January 2015